Arthur Llewellyn

The Real and Ideal

Arthur Llewellyn

The Real and Ideal

ISBN/EAN: 9783337049782

Printed in Europe, USA, Canada, Australia, Japan

Cover: Foto ©Andreas Hilbeck / pixelio.de

More available books at **www.hansebooks.com**

THE REAL AND IDEAL.

POEMS

BY

ARTHUR LLEWELLYN

LONDON:
HURST AND BLACKETT, PUBLISHERS,
13, GREAT MARLBOROUGH STREET.
1863.

CONTENTS.

CONTENTS.

THE REAL AND IDEAL.

THE SPIRIT OF POESY.

PART I.

I.

SPIRIT, that when the world was young,
  Didst wander o'er the plains of Earth,
  And waken into tones of mirth
Her dull grey heart; like harp new-strung.

Of land, sea, sky, not one was mute,
  Naiads along the rills divine
  Laughed lightly, and the happy Nine
Sang to Apollo's silver lute.

Oh, thou wert ever hovering o'er
  The minds of mortals, in the days
  When cloudlets beamed with Iris' rays,
And Neptune moaned on every shore;—

When Flora strewed the way with flowers,
  Though 'neath lurked Hades' gloomy bed;
  And hurling thunderbolts o'erhead
Sate Jove august, supreme of powers;—

Imagination dimmed the Real;
  And thou wert seen in calm and storm—
  No idle tale, but living form;
Man's spirit dwelt in the Ideal!

II.

We see not Iris in the cloud,
  Nor Gods to old Parnassus climb;
  They've passed away from Earth—and Time
Hath wrapped Age round them like a shroud.

The world is no more young—"*It seems*,"
  Is changed into "*It is*"—The Life,
  That pants and throbs in weary strife,
Will never more be lulled by dreams.

Dwellest thou, Spirit, with the cold
  Stern Present, this, we call our own ?
  Or by the grey sepulchral stone
Still watchest at the grave of Old ?

III.

Thou that didst open to the Blind
  The gates of Paradise, where he
  Saw in the Past the bright " *To be*,"
Glassed there in glory undefined!

Like to the softened light of Even,
  When winds have ceased to vex the sea,
  Came o'er my soul the thought of thee ;—
A calm—which seemed a dream of Heaven:

I sought thee through green wood and glen,
  And mountain crag, a joyous child ;
  And in late years through mazes wild
Amid the noisy haunts of Men.

Among the opening buds of Spring,
  I saw the light prints of thy feet,—
  Heard lingering echoes, rich and sweet,
As of thy voice through forests ring :—

3   B 2

IV.

Have watched from noon to even's wane,
  On summer's waving sea of grass,
  The shadows, lengthening as they pass,
Till lost in gloom along the plain :—

When rich old Autumn, crownèd King,
  Laughed at the yellow-tasselled grain
  Fighting and battling with the rain ;
While warrior winds roared wondering;

The merry old King, laughing, died ;
  And treacherous blithe wily Day
  Became the sworn friend of Decay,
  And like tiger-whelps at play
They gambolled on the mountain's side.

When Death's keen terror-spreading gale
  Swept the tall trees, and brown leaves fell ;
  Cold tear-drops through the tangled dell
Trickled adown the branches pale ;—

And flowers dare not venture forth,
  For far and near along the wold,
  In swift cloud-chariot dark and cold,
Rode the strong Tyrant of the North.

From the rose-blush to frosty rime,
  With Hope, my guardian Angel still,
  I waited for thy Spirit-thrill
While added years were lost to Time.

v.

'Twas pleasant through Night's pathless way
  To watch the moon glide forth alone;
  When nought was heard save owl's sad tone,
Or through the mist the watch-dog's bay,—

Or hail the light in Eastern sky,
  The first faint streak of rising day
  Tinge the horizon's line of grey,
And morning ope its dazzling eye,—

Or con the page of bardic lore,
  At noon beside some pebbly brook,
  In a sequestered shady nook,
And think of Spirits gone before.

Often, while wandering in the bright
  Warm Summer, on the tawny sands,
  I thought thy home in other lands
Must be beyond my bounded sight ;—

VI.

Youth loves the far off—yes, 'tis strange
  That it should love a foreign shore,
  Ever see sunlight playing o'er
The distant hills, and long for change :—

And roving Fancy's home for thee
  Was in some tranquil fairy grove,
  Sacred to Liberty and Love,
Where shades of Genius hover free.

Perchance where from the heaving blue
  Green isles make glad the seaman's sight ;
  Where night seems but a paler light,
And Fragrance wakes to drink the dew.

Or o'er the crested azure wave,
  Where low the sun sinks in the west,
  Where rich-hued cloudlets brood, and rest
Above the spot Day finds a grave.

VII.

What words shall paint the Infant's joy
  When first, in wonder and delight,
  It hails Earth's blossoms bathed in light,
Earth's roses, ere the thorns alloy?

6

Oh, mark it gaily trip along ;—
  Treading the spangled grassy sod,
  Fairest of all the works of God,
Music each sound, each thought a song.

As mind expands—reflection grows,—
  "Who made that bud with dew-gems wet?"
  "Yon flaming sun above who set?"—
Such questions break the Soul's repose.

Sing on, ye birds !—wave, ye green leaves !—
  Each breeze that blows its influence spreads,
  Oh, world, mar not the beauteous threads,
That web of thought, the infant weaves !

VIII.

When mocking Doubt hath spread its snare,
  And Unbelief approving smiles,
  Haste to the spot beloved erewhiles,
Where first thy young lips lisped a prayer ;—

Retrace in thought the winding way
  That led thee from a mother's knee,
  The lingering beams of Infancy
Will serve to light the darksome way ;—

And thou shalt list and hear again
　　Music that through the wide air floats,
　　Sweet as some quiring Angel's notes ;—
Though Reason cold may sneer as vain :

With Faith the soul shall wing its flight,—
　　Barriers Philosophy hath taught,
　　Like frost-work, beautifully wrought,
Shall melt 'neath rays of Heavenly light.

IX.

As on a mountain's topmost height
　　Some tiny pool, with silver eye,
　　Mirrors the planet vast on high,
Far up the deep dark arch of Night ;

The Soul that spurns timidity,
　　Above the chance and change of Time,
　　Merges all in the great, sublime,
And mirrors the Infinity ;—

The Man whose childish feet have trod
　　With fearless step the mountain path,
　　And made high rocks his play-place, hath
Some grand conception of a God !

8

The memory of wood-draped hills,—
  The distant tinkling of sheep-bell—
  In after-years, as in the shell
Its glad home music—the heart fills.

x.

When eyes are closed to outward forms,—
  When Care's tide ebbs, and rest is given,
  The Spirit, lark-like, soars to Heaven,
And sings above the warring storms.

(Alone we delve into our minds,
  Learn what we were, and what we are,
  Recount each victory—each scar,
Each wound that time with healing binds;

Each joy—but can we be *alone?*
  Those we call *dead*—are they not near?
  "*Alone!*" oh, word dreaded or dear,
Still with a sadness in its tone!)

'Twas night—still Thought its vigils kept,
  While, like a ship by breezes fanned,
  That far behind her leaves the land,
All, all things faded, and I slept.

9

XI.

Oh, but it was a glorious dream!
  The spirit-forms of ancient days
  Rose up before me ; and the lays
Of seers and prophets—like a stream

Borne by the breath of all the years,
  That backward rolled the heaving tide ;
  Until its surges, echoing wide,
Rang holy music in mine ears.

As though, in an Enchanter's glass,
  Araby's wilderness I saw ;
  And, trembling, heard with soul-filled awe
Old Sinai quake, Jehovah pass ;

Beheld the remnant warriors flee—
  Heard blend the shouts on Gideon's plain
  With wail of mourners o'er the slain,
'' The smile of God was victory."

Lebanon's groves with praises rang;
  The flocks upon the mountain's side
  Browse peacefully—young fingers glide
O'er tuneful harp-chords—David sang.

Beheld descend through parted sky
　　Fire-chariots, and Elijah rose
　　Deathless to Heaven—the blue veil close
And tranquil clouds go sailing by.

Then heard resounding through the years
　　Voices on Zion's crumbling wall ;
　　Isaiah to repentance call—
And Jeremiah wet with tears.

XII.

Another scene—a placid sea—
　　A fisher's boat—with cheerful will
　　The nets are cast, the winds are still,
The stars look down on Galilee.

A voice floats on the air of night,
　　It is the *Teacher's*—there sits He,
　　The Christ that was, is, is to be,
The link where God and man unite.

Softly the vision passed away,
　　Shining amid the waters blue :
　　It glided, glided from my view—
Still glowing like the sun's last ray.

11

XIII.

Then I was in a noisome court,
  Where pain and festering disease,
  In a mazy dance that did not cease,
Went round with human life to sport.

And one came forth, and bade them look
  At the yawning gulf beneath,
  Ere Death drew from its reeking sheath
The keen-edged sword which o'er them shook ;

And one led a child, pale and wan,
  From out the shadow dark, to see
  The light that shone o'er grass and tree,
And smiled in love on fallen man.

And Poesy seemed whispering *there*—
  The child was taught, at even-time,
  To list the old Cathedral chime
Peal through the murky atmosphere.

XIV.

And there was a mother—a widowed one—
  She rocked her sickly babe to sleep
  With strains of woe so wild and deep,
As though she wished Life's sands were run.

I looked where Misery had wrought
   Such fearful havoc, leagued with wrong,
   Where Right was trampled by the throng,
And Truth had left the human thought.

Then, with a loud and sudden rush,
   A flood was sweeping all away —
   When, climbing up a rocky way,
A faintness and a dreamy hush

Crept o'er my spirit—I awoke ;
   Not in the pleasant eastern clime,
   Nor on the hills of Childhood's time,
But 'mid a City's noise and smoke.

PART II.

I.

Faith, Hope, and Love, a glorious three—
   Or one—whose talismanic power
   Saves the possessor in the hour—
The evil hour of Misery !

Faith, Hope, and Love, when storm-winds hurled
  Destruction, like a mighty foe,
  Sweeping the beauteous earth below—
A Deluge rolled above the world ;

Safe from the waves, within the Ark,
  Ye rested with old Noah's soul,
  Until he reached Ararat's goal,
Then glowed amid the cloudlet dark.

And yet ye are ideal—oh, high
  Bright rainbow ladder, richly given
  For us to reach and climb to Heaven.
Evanish never from our sky !

II.

Why hopeless tread the shades of Life ?
  Why walk as though among the dead ?
  Why give the hungry stones for bread,
With cruel words that stir up strife ?

There is more poetry in one
  Poor heart ; in one hot scalding tear—
  One withered smile, though cold and sere,
Than all 'neath Heaven the glorious Sun

14

Beholds of earth, mount, waterfall—
　Ocean's wide wealth of isles o'ercast
　With time-strewn records of the Past—
One human life outweighs them all.

Life! with its meed of hopes and cares,
　Its crown of thorns, or wreath of flowers,
　That, borne by the light-footed hours,
O'ertake and leave us unawares.

Life, with awakened conscience stings—
　Life, with remorse and vain regrets ;
　Duty, with its uncancelled debts—
All that Man's tortured bosom wrings !

Mistrust, the Sceptic's stumbling-block—
　Dark Vice, with all its hideous brood ;
　Evil contrasted with the Good—
Life's shoals and quicksands, with the rock ;

Vice's wintry desolation—and
　The summer freshness goodness spreads
　Through the warm heart, like glittering threads
Of streams meandering through green land ;

Valour, with manly bravery
  Bearing its cross, and ne'er cast down;
  Victory with its glossy crown ;
And sinking shackled Slavery.

Indifference, with its poppy wreath,
  Enthusiasm's glowing ray—
  Wild Speculation's shadow play—
Hypocrisy, with tainted breath.

Love, Mirth, and Joy—a happy group ;
  Mild Pity, furious bitter Hate ;
  And Envy, hissing at the gate—
Where rest gay Pleasure's merry troop.

Or holy Faith's seraphic wings,
  Soaring beyond Time's busy hours—
  These are the strong and lofty powers
Which now must strike the Idalian strings.

Whate'er the heart may feel or know
  Of grief, or pain's deep piercing dart ;
  Or anguish's self-consuming smart,
Whate'er of joy, or blackest woe.

16

III.

" The Shades of Life,"—the people throng
   Together, questioning if above
   Still dwelleth He, the God of Love?
Trembling, they grope through blackest wrong.

The holy mountain, cloaked with mist,
   May straight before their vision rise;
   But still the legate of the skies
Comes not with comfort to the midst.

Those wanderers in a thirsty land
   Of old beheld the stubborn rock
   Tremble, and yield beneath the shock
Of a frail rod in Moses' hand.

Lo ! sparkling gushed a living rill
   Of crystal waters cool and free;
   The Moses-rod of *Sympathy*
We have—ay, use it as we will.

IV.

From the rose-blush to frosty rime—
   O Poesy! I sought thee still;
   Sought thee o'er glen, and copse, and hill,
While added years were lost to time!

17   C

Nor knew that thou wert here alway ;
  While yet my truant steps would roam,
  Thou, like an Angel in our home,
Hallowest the common *Everyday*.

A presence felt, although *unseen*;
  Nor missed, until its upward flight
  Sinks on the soul in gloom and night,
And sadness gathers o'er the scene.

Like to a sun, in Winter's sky,
  Hidden by many a fold of cloud,
  Though mists our feeble sight o'ershroud—
Still brightly burns the sun on high !

V.

Yes, though the World is growing old,
  With brow austere, and heart unkind,
  And breath harsh as the wintry wind
That blows along the barren wold.

The Beautiful is living still,
  Undimmed the clear cerulean blue ;
  Unpaled the soft sweet verdant hue
That wreathes the plain, and robes the hill.

Grandly the woods wave to and fro,
　　Their ancient anthems in the trees;
　　Chant those wild minstrels, winds and leaves,
As in the ages long ago,—

In glorious lustre as of yore,
　　Bright stars be-gem the swarthy night,
　　From orient seas Day rises bright,
Prism-hued waves leap on the shore.

And ever in the murkiest gloom
　　Some gleam of light breaks on our way;
　　Still beaming o'er the dim life-day,
Gilding the death-night of the tomb.

Ever remains *some* joy to bless
　　The sorrow of the darkest grief;
　　Ever *some* angel of relief,
Oases in each wilderness.

VI.

The presence of th' Immortal God
　　Hallows each spot of this green earth;
　　And Soul, a gem of priceless worth,
Glitters in radiance through its clod.

If that which Thou hast made t' outlive
The oldest star, with prying eyes,
Seek glimpses of that Paradise,
Veiled o'er by Thee—O God forgive!

If the weak, the diminutive—
The Atom rise and seek to scan
Thy wondrous law, thy mighty plan—
Question the All-wise—God forgive!

All fabled glory, howe'er bright,
Fades in the lustre of Truth's day;
Extinguished, like a taper's ray
In summer's golden blaze of light.

VII.

Could we with noble energy,
And with a watch-man's practised eye,
Survey wild Being surging by,
The quivering of that human sea;

In thunder-tones would bid us rise—
And ever linger not amid
Dead sapless leaves, by blossoms hid,
Where Beauties tattered Truths despise.

Tempests may lour upon the hill—
  Billows convulsed roar in the storm;
  Hearts bleed, cheeks blanch, Poesy's form,
Christ-like, through tumult, cries, "Be still!"

The Heaven-born binds around the brow
  The glossy leaves, the laurel wreath,
  And from all future thunders safe,
It rests, unharmed by ills below.

VIII.

Is Life not bliss?   We dare not tell
  The sorrow-stricken that it *is*,—
  To him in Misery's abyss,
'Twere mockery to say—" All's well."

Yet "Life *is* bliss," and Death alone
  Is the *all* dark, *all* sad, *all* drear;
  Then what is that men call "Despair,"
That blank from which all hope is gone?

We know not—but this know, scenes *near*,
  That crushed, appalled us—*distant*, have
  A pleasant hue—beyond the grave—
Dark "now," perchance, will bright appear.

IX.

Spirit of Poesy ! sweep the lyre
  With gentle touch—as breezes wake
  The Æolian strings, and music make—
With words touch as with holy fire

The lips of those who, Jacob-like,
  Would win a blessing from thee here—
  Whose hero-hearts, unchained by fear,
In moral warfare pant to strike !

Who go from Happiness, and mark
  The never-happy—ay, whose lips
  Breathe comfort through the dire eclipse—
Wing thoughts, like lightning, through the dark !

X.

The spirit Poesy moves and dwells,
  Not only on the purple heath,
  All fragrant with the broom-trees' breath—
Or in old woods, whose rise and swells

Make noon-day twilight ;—(earthly *things*
  Though all magnificent) to mould
  A brother-tie (not one of gold)
'Twixt *Man* and *Man*, her flight she wings,

And calls to aid her all the Powers ;
　And weaves bright links of love, to bind
　In harmony all, all mankind ;
And scatters o'er this world of ours

Blossoms of joy unknown before :
　Noblest of creeds—whose creed is this,
　" The law of Kindness," Law of Bliss—
Faith, Hope, and Love for evermore.

XI.

'Tis not alone where Beauty reigns,
　And, blissful as a lark in June,
　Joy ever sings his sweetest tune,
Where no sad echoes mock the strains ;—

'Tis not alone where all is fair,
　Where flowers of richest hues are found—
　And fountains flash with ringing sound,
Amid the glad, the light, and rare.

The strains of Poesy should be,—
　But in the homes of Poor and Low,
　Whispering hope and soothing woe,
Setting Sin's abject bondsmen free—

Smoothing the wrinkled brow of Care;
Smiling with Splendour and with Wealth,
The couch of Sickness—glow of Health;
Ay, breeze-like, floating everywhere!

XII.

Where Ignorance broods, cloud-like, oer—
And Gloom and Superstition blind,
Torture and haunt the fear-tost mind—
A chaos wild without a shore;

Where Want and Sin, companions old—
(Want goeth first) knock at the heart,
And enter in to gall and smart—
Till Love's last embers e'en grow cold;

Where Crime and Ruin, 'neath their ban,
Shadow the few faint rays of light;
Like evil angels of the night,
Wrestle and grapple with the Man;

The claims of Human brotherhood,
And Charity, with sov'reign string,
Mild Poesy should teach and sing—
The harbinger of endless good—

XIII.

To Misery bringing fortitude—
  Kind hope unto the branded name—
  Mercy to Guilt in chains and shame—
Peopling the loneliest solitude

With angel-forms—a glorious throng!
  The freshness of primeval youth
  To Man returns again; and Truth,
With music, leads the soul along;

Dropping like showers of summer rain
  On the parched, sterile, arid clay:
  All light, all hope—welcome as day;
All joy—and all that these contain.

XIV.

No cold majestic pyramid;
  Ancient, imposing, vast, and bold;
  Bearing the bones of monarchs old—
Or where old relics rich are hid;

No sculptured marble's stately air
  To startle the deep-wondering sense—
  Standing in calm magnificence,
Deathly serene—placidly fair—

Poesy needs :—but Life, true Life—
　With quick vibrations of heart-chords
　Thrilling through glowing thoughts and words,
Where Sympathy and Love are rife.

XV.

Sweet words, that seem like bells to chime,
　Through the old halls of Memory—
　And waken echoing melody,
Linking eternity to time !

The flowers that bloom ; the birds that sing ;
　The tranquil nights and happy days—
　The halo-light of love which plays
Around Home's hallowed fairy ring ;—

Warm breathing, feeling, flesh and blood—
　Still hoping for a better land,
　With which each man may clasp a hand,
And claim a cordial brotherhood.

XVI.

We need no ghosts of other years—
　No hero-myth or demi-god—
　No bolt at a celestial nod,
To thunder through the rolling spheres.

No mighty giant of the North,
  Hammer to wield or strike a blow;
  No Jotun swift from land of snow,
In his ice-ship to wander forth.

The ghosts of other years may sleep—
  The Present, with a step sublime,
  Stalks o'er their graves: the while old Time
Rocks them in slumber still more deep.

XVII.

Spirit, that when the world was young,
  Didst wander o'er the plains of Earth,
  And waken into tones of mirth
Her dull grey heart, like harp new-strung,—

The living Immortality,
  Radiant with untold glory bright,
  Robed round with a celestial light—
We, being mortal, cannot see.

Come, Spirit, viewless as the wind,
  Lead us, and we will soar with thee,
  Away through far Immensity,
On the light pinions of the Mind—

27

Soar e'en to where Heaven's portals shine ;
  Hear echoes of the anthem high
  Ring through the wide arch of the sky—
Some measure of the life divine !

Seer, that with divinest art,
  See'st merit thro' rags torn and old ;
  And vileness oft thro' silken fold—
And beauty in a dull weed's heart !

Teach me, amid the giddy whirl,
  Foam-waves have hid from happier eyes,
  To dive and seize the glorious prize
In Life's deep tide, and find the pearl ;

With patient faith, e'en from our youth,
  The thrones of Ignorance and Night
  Ever to assail with arms of Right,
And the bare sword of mighty Truth.

O'ermastered by no passing storm—
  Still walk abreast with the glad years,
  With no vain unavailing fears ;—
Unshackled by dead creeds and forms,

28

Tread the rough path—where Wrong and Strife,
  Like lions fierce, block up the way,
  And Joy's warm sunbeams seldom play,
And learn the mystery of Life!

NIGHT.

High up the eastern heavens, great flocks of clouds,
Like swarthy birds that herald darkness, flap
Their broad and dusky wings :—Deep silence rests
On Earth ; while Nature waits the approach of night.
Shadowy, solemn Night ! With mystic touch
Waking the slumbering chords of melody
Within my soul ; My very pulses throb
With fervent adoration to my God ;
When thou, O Night ! from thy far wanderings
In ether's wilderness, returnest here—
Returnest, like an exiled king, to claim
Again thy glittering crown of stars.

30

The distant hum hath died away ;
The trampling turmoil and wild strife of life
Forgotten for awhile, in peaceful rest
The million-peopled City sleeps ;—and, save
A few who will or dare not sleep—all rest.
Sweet sleep ! Foretaste of that long tranquil night,
The tired clay shall slumber through, when Soul,
Untrammelled with the things of Time,
Shall mount to heavenly regions, known alone
To God, his angels, and redeemed saints—
Shall mount aloft—or sink !
Oh, happy Sleep ! calm counterfeit of Death—
Silence protects thee from the strife of tongues ;
Twin Charity and Hope thy guardians are,
While meek-eyed Peace lays her smooth cheek on thine,
Her cooling palm upon thy feverish brow—
And stills the throbbings of the o'erburdened brain.

Daylight is gone—The landscape fades away—
Oblivion closes over outward things ;
Chains all the Man, except his chainless mind—
Mind, Heart, Will, Soul, ay, call it what thou wilt,
Active as the eternal universe—
Yokefellow to the body—Oh, how strong !

31

How lofty, how sublime when free!
Running wild riot in the spacious halls
That ope upon Infinitude!
Imagination revels there, amid
The cloud-fields of Dream-land—Enchanted ground;
Where clam'rous Care is dumb—and even Grief
Forgets to weep;—Where Doubt is Certainty;
Hope, Realisation—Poverty, Wealth.—
Whose soothing air can calm the bursting pangs
Of wild Despair, and change Captivity
To Freedom—There, ay, and there alone, Past,
Present, Future meet—Where the Hours pause
In their gay circling dance—and Time itself
Is an Eternity. Fame, Honour, Love,
Power—each, and all, gladden the Dreamer's soul,
As some sea-swell the parched and thirsty sand,
Waves have long left.

      The moonlight glimmers on the sward;
A holy radiance—Circling the dim night,
Like mercy o'er the darkened path of Life—
Pale Cynthia! blest by many a heart,
That in unrest, like the foam-crested surge,
Panting for peace along the dreary beach,

Looks up to her—Kind Moon ! she bringeth to
The Seaman's mind, in midnight's lonely watch,
A pleasant picture—Waving trees, through which
The pale light gleams upon a little cot—
The one poor cot in all the wealthy world,
The wanderer may call "*Home*,"—The Invalid
Smiles a wan welcome as the cheering rays
Stream through the lattice-pane;—And to the eyes
Of the fast-sinking dying one it comes,
Peopled with Light-tiared angel-bands—
Heaven's convoy, that shall lead him to a land
Needing nor Sun, nor Moon, nor Star.

                    It is the dead of night;
Huge Evil rears his giant form ; summons
His scattered hosts again ; and, brandishing
His deadly weapons o'er th' unconscious world,
Vows *endless* war with Good—omnipotent,
Eternal Good !—See, sweeping through the air
Methinks they come (or is it fantasy ?) :
Swifter than tempest's wing, tumultuously
They come !—Murder, with pale ghosts at his side :
Pride, furious Revenge, Wrong, Avarice,
Base Perfidy, snake-like hissing Envy,—

With all their trains;—what frenzied shrieks, what yells!
Was e'er such discord?   Earth, O Earth! and wilt?
And canst thou harbour monsters foul as these?
Thou, the Immortal one of old pronounced
To be, ay, "very good"—And angels, through
Eternity's bright portal, smiled upon
With joy, to see thee roll through space, and take
Thy place among the worlds; and chorus with
The morning stars the glorious song that broke
The bonds of captive Silence.   Earth, O Earth!
Has Evil fixed his throne on thy green hills?
And made thy woods and vales his dwelling-place?
And drowned with his loud roar thy chant of joy?
—Ha! there they go—a legion, *his* fierce band;
Skeleton Death goes hurrying after—
Ruin following closely in his track;—
They've passed, lost in the distant gloom; they've passed;
And yet their hateful voices ring, and rend
The silence of the dark concave of Night!

But there's *more* Good than Evil in the world;
Ay, laugh, ye fiends! and sneer, ye infidels!
But there're *less* thorns than flowers—The Enemy
Sows tares; but Oh! a rich ripe harvest will

The Angel reapers garner up in Heaven!

                                                        All silently,
The sullen clouds are driven by ruthless
Blasts across the midnight sky—As sere leaves
Before the desolating autumn winds;
The half-formed Moon hastens upon her way,
Like a fond parent, leading by the hand
Her favourite little star.—

How still! how calm! no sound is heard,
No sound save distant roar of waters far,
In the shell-paved deep caverns of the sea,
Rousing faint Echo on the dreary shore;—
There stand the hoary patriarchal rocks,
As they have stood for ages, listening
To the sweet prattle of bright infant waves,
That play with their long grey locks of sea-weed:
They seem to smile now, in the dim moonlight,—
But when the vexed surge leaps and foams with rage,
Fearful the frowns on those time-furrowed brows!

      The waves are rocked to sleep—the winds
Have sung their lullaby—*they*, too, have slept—
But yonder lingers still some Zephyr lone,

Weaving its fingers soothingly, amid
The sombre trellis of the ivy leaves——

But, hark! the Winds
Are sighing heavily—they have gone down
The beach—and whispered something to the waves,
See! one by one they start from sleep—and now
Are dancing to and fro;—Above, the wan,
Pale terror-stricken Moon, still paler grown,
With that lone star, flees from the storm—closely
Pursued by wingèd lightnings swift—and from
Yon mighty ebon cloud I hear the sound
Of muttered thunder!

Louder it roars! rocking
The earth as 'twould unrest the sleeping Dead
Of ages.   Deep hollow groans, from moaning
Winds, convulse the gulfs and chasms where brooding
Silence dwells; The fluttering sea-gulls shriek,
And, blind with terror, dash against the rocks!

Fiercer, and fiercer,
The wild storm rages on—as if it fain
Would pierce the inmost depths of this dark globe;
A sheet of living fire lights up the skies!

The lightning quivers tangled in the clouds,
Ghastly the glare reflected on the waves !
The air above gleams like a glassy sea,
Burning with sunset's gold and crimson glow ;
The rumbling Thunder-car rolls on, and on—
Showering down darkness : deep, deeper, now
Profound as an eclipse through space——
              Ha ! there's another flash !

SPRING TIME.

PART I.

I.

Soft as the breath of Love,
Spring, thou dost ever move
Among the churchyard trees ;—
Bending above the silent bed,
Shaking thy crown of leaves ;—
Canst smile where sleep the Dead ?
The yew weeps tears of blood,
Ever in sorrowing mood ;
But thou, in sportive glee,
Wilt wreathe gay flowers above the sod,
And bring to the dull Clay
Smiles from the bright Day-god ;—

Oh, sure the spirit comes to view
This spot ; then set the violet,
And all that's sweet above the grave ; Why plant the
yew ?

II.

With a leafy mantle clad,
Thou makest old Earth glad ;—
Zephyrs the blossoms fan,
And all, in joy and wild delight,
Mock the dark gloom of Man—
All else is blissful, bright ;
He, he alone beneath the sky,
From thee can borrow thoughts of sorrow—
Spring, even thou canst bring the moisture to his eye.

III.

Memory, from her caves,
Goeth amid the graves
Of the Past abysmal ;
And readeth on the gleaming stones,
That ghostly and dismal
Stand 'bove the buried bones ;

That Winter, dark and cold,
Hath hidden 'neath the mould
The ones I loved, from me ;
Autumn hath brought me many a grief—
But, sweet Spring, I love thee!
Thou com'st to my relief;
Attuning wild Despair to mirth—
And telling me from each green tree,
That there is Happiness and joy yet left on earth.

IV.

Thou art the same old Spring
That used to chirp and sing,
As if for very bliss,
That a thing like thee, so fresh and fair,
Lived in a world like this,
Harassed by pain and care ;
Blithe as Day, the same old Spring,
With sunny ray, and lightsome play,
That to my ear, in Childhood, used to chirp and sing !

V.

Sad is it with the Blind,
In prison dark confined—

Sight cannot rove where leaves
Weave robes, in which bare woods are drest,
Nor where the blue sky heaves
Through clouds that will not rest;—
The daisied path along the hill
He cannot find,—Sad to be blind!
But the *Mind* with clouded vision, oh, sadder still!

VI.

There are who never know
The purifying glow,
The freshness thou canst bring—
Whose iron hearts corrode with rust;
Life's tree, unblossoming,
Is thick with Traffic's dust:
The parched, lone wayside flower
Awaits a welcome hour,
When the awakening rain
Will sing along the meadow grass,
And o'er the dusky plain,—
But for those, alas! alas!
What gentle showers shall lave
Hearts hard and cold with the blight of Gold?
Awake the dull ear, earthy, earthy as the Grave!

VII.

Oh, how I thank the Powers,
That in Life's morning hours,
Guided my soul to love
Beauty and Good;—Twin Genii they,
Bright guardians from above;
Moving amid the day;
Haunting the Twilight stilly,—
Calm and fair, floating everywhere;
O'er tree-top high, and low beside the water-lily.

PART II.

I.

What is the World?—Its islands and its oceans,
Its mountains crowned with everlasting snow,
Its rushing cataracts, wakening emotions
Ecstatic as they flow?
Are they realities?—Flower-spangled
Meads, and thickets tangled—
And all the gorgeous pictures Nature hath
To deck our darksome path—

Lighting us through the days of Infancy,
Moving about us in eternal joy;
    Till dreams of mystic glory
Halo our spirits;—Nothing can destroy
    Those raptures visionary,
That haunt us as we go; Still questioning
Truth of each bright created thing;
    The Why? the Wherefore? Whither?
    The answer ever—"Thither."
The fiery spark, The Intellectual gleam
Within us, whispers,—"Life is *not* a dream."

II.

On, on perpetually, the Seasons urge
Young Spring; mild Summer; weary Autumn pale;—
Then we hear midnight moan the dead year's dirge,
    Year, dead in Winter's Vale,—
    Ever changing; yet changeless ever;—
    Like some broad rolling river,
Or as the varying cloudlets fleet
    In passing, still repeat
The vanished forms and hues of yesterday;
Thus still, the Past, Sunshine, and foliage green,
    Hours swept away,

Return again—Splendour and light to dance
　　Upon the Present's way.—
The last year's music—distant strain,
Through leafy woods echoes again ;
　　　　Skies, that erst wore leaden hue,
　　　　Now robed in ethereal blue—
The same tints glowing in the waving flowers ;
Our hearts exclaim—Lo ! these are *last* year's bowers !

III.

How came they here, with fragrant breath
Wafting sweet incense o'er the dewy leas ?
Methought they passed the gloomy porch of Death,
　　　　Crossing Oblivion's seas
　　　　Into the tomb of Being—
　　　　Far, far beyond all seeing ;
And there, safe from the tempest's sullen roar,
　　　　Rested for evermore ;—
　　　　I marked the clouds drop many a tear,
　　　　As each bright blossom drooped its weary head ;
　　　　And o'er its chilly bier,—
Like some old Minstrel over Chieftain dead,
　　　　The Wind through forests drear,

Struck its wild harp; oft uttering a groan—
Wandering o'er cheerless moor and fell alone;—
Lorn fountains, hills, and groves,
Once more behold your loves!
Wreathed with gay smiles the sunlight plays upon,
Ye dreamed of anguish—See! they are not gone :—

IV.

But ah! 'mid the returning joys of Earth,
So beautiful! 'mid brooklet's rippling song,
I miss loved voices, silvery tones of mirth,
That ever gladsome throng!
Why come they not? Earth, call *them* back;
Bid them return from last year's track;
Lost Friends, clear stars of purity, love-bright;
Gone down in trackless gloom;—
Vain man! Why mourn? Soon shall *thy* Reason's might
Depart;—Such our sad doom!

V.

Beneath yon eaves there was a vacant nest;
The bird had taken wing—
Flown, none knew whither;—Now, with panting breast,

45

I hear him twittering,
His home new-tenanting;—
But *long* shall wait the desolated home,
Of him who passed the undiscovered bourne!

VI.

Blessed Word of Life!   Hope of the life *to be!*
Saviour, thrice glorified! Erring Soul's Friend!
Who taught dark wondering Humanity
     Death's waking knows no end;—
    Ever revivifying Earth
    Might tell dead Winter's vernal birth;
Ten thousand ages see that glorious sun
    Its heavenly journey run;
    Yet leave Man's hungering soul forlorn,
    Existence tell him he was mortal—
    But show no dawning morn—
    Point to no hand could ope the prison's portal,
    And raise the mouldered form;
Had not the holy Word breathed from on high,
    Proclaimed a Spring-time nigh—
    When, like yon budding tree,
    Man second birth shall see;
And, flower-like, burst the Grave's dull shadow deep;
For *Death*, with all its terrors, is but *Sleep*.

PART III.

I.

It is a noble thought, to feel, to view
Each atom of the Universe, each fair
Expanding tree; blossoms of mantling hue,
    Wafting their perfumed air
     O'er Earth and sky; each living thing—
      From fluttering butterfly of Spring,
       To the wild Eagle, with keen steadfast gaze
       Eyeing the sun's bright blaze;—
Through wide Intelligence's vast, wondrous scale;
From Instinct to the lofty heights of Soul,
    And Immortality—
   Each one a link of that great whole,
     Being's mysterious chain—
Vibrating from the cloud-veiled dazzling throne,
    Glory's meridian,—
    To feel through Day's delight,
    And the deep silent Night,
Throughout Nature's greatest and minutest part,
Soul, like the throbbing pulse of a great heart!

47

II.

But Nature, to me, is one vast Poem ;—Sublime
Ideas of the Godhood ; brightly woven
Throughout Creation, in harmonious prime
        Of unity—Given
      In light resplendent, to illume
      With glory, the Soul's darksome gloom ;—
And blest ! is the unclouded mental sight
      Can read its page aright—
    Guide the exulting Spirit's soaring wing
Through the deep boundless space ; With sacred power,
      Sweep the impassioned string
   Of Inspiration's harp ; and tower
      To Truth's majestic Spring !
Lift subtle thought, and joyous roll away
      The haze that dims our noontide ray;—
        Awhile forget that tears
        E'er dimmed the shrouded Years;
Forget it is the whispering breeze you hear,
Think 'tis the echo of the Angel quire !

III.

The waving pines, on yonder mountain high,
Seem listening to the Zephyr's holy psalm ;

Now bending to the vale, now to the sky
　　　　With its eternal calm,
　　　　Uplifting their green arms—
　　　　Silence, each leaflet charms;
As though that cloudless firmament above,
　　　　Intensely blue, smiling in love,
Bade them be still. Look up, thou soul of mine;
See, though wild winds hurled many a frowning cloud
　　　　O'er that clear sky—while through Time
Each young year fluttered;—Darkness, like a shroud
　　　　Hath gathered; yet doth it shine
Unruffled as when Adam's wondering eyes
　　　　Oped in the bowers of Paradise;
　　　　　　And thus, though troubles may
　　　　　　Obscure the Heart's bright day,
Dark shadows overhang Hope's glorious portal,
Soul, calm be thou!—Thou art Immortal!

IV.

When one by one the stars put out their light,
And Morning drew the curtain of the skies;
Startling that lingering dreamer, ebon Night—
　　　　I saw the Lark arise,

Brush his dewy wing, and go
From bed of king-cups yellow,
To welcome in the richness Spring discloses ;
Violets, cowslips, pale primroses,—
Earth's sparkling stars of hope ; The blythe lark sang
Carolling music, showering peal on peal,
Throughout the wide air rang
A thrill of joy ; methought 'twas an appeal
To the mute heart of man.
Birds, insects, bees, God's meanest works rejoice—
Fountains, rills, flowerets, find a voice,—
That cloud-lost speck pours forth his happiness,
As though he *never* could express
The bliss he feels ; soaring and singing there,
Seeking for heaven throughout the fields of air.

V.

Here, deep within this foliage-shaded glen,
The Heart re-treads the pathway of the years
Towards sweet hallowed days ; Gladness again
Chases away all tears,—
Joy smiles upon the death of Sorrow ;
Gilding the sunnier morrow

With the golden tints of glowing youth—
    Radiant as Truth !—
The Angel, Peace, is smiling on me now,
        Sweet smiles of beauty—Spirits in the flowers.
        As the cool breezes kiss my brow,
Waft me to other scenes, to bygone hours !—
        The suns, moons, stars, of " long ago,"
Are ever bright, its seasons ever vernal—
        Its worship, thoughts of the Eternal—
        The faces there are ever young ;
        Its friends still fond, its songs still sung ;—
There, fadeless the bright wreath Affection wove ;
One serene Day !—One holy dream of Love !

O, THERE ARE SOUNDS OF MYSTIC MELODY.

O, there are sounds of mystic melody
   By unseen voices softly breathed from heaven,
   When twilight faintly sighs his last "good even,"
As on its stem each flower hangs heavily :—
   It soothes the musing Poet's pensive heart ;
   Cold disappointment, and keen sorrow's smart
No more are felt ; while round, above him, hover
   A busy brood of thoughts ; With silken wings
   Fanning the mind's deep silence : As on Spring's
Warm days, when butterflies would fain discover
   The violet's eye—bright hue of sky and ocean—
   Its balmy odour guides their fluttering motion—
The Poet's spirit, fancy-led, pursues
The fairy path that leads him to the Muse.

Wan, pale-browed Sorrow may sit by him oft—
    Twining with fingers soft her cypress wreath;
    But clouds that shadow the dark world beneath,
Show silver linings when he soars aloft;—.
    Envy may tempt him with the bauble gold,
    And Want, with feeble voice so faint and cold,
Whisper of woes unnumbered—say he *must*
    Fetter that ever-roving heaven-born mind;
    Bind that proud spirit—subtle as the wind,
And grind that magic Thought to *useful dust*.
    But oh, those voices, breathing through the night.
    Waft him to Paradise on pinions light!
His is a noble heritage—Kind Fate
Smile on him!—Guardian Genii round him wait!

THE AWAKENING OF LIBERTY.

LIGHT 'mid the world's dark shadows! Through the
    clouds
Outbursting with a rosy halo; as when Morn
Peers from the folds of her Night-Mother's shroud—
    Smiling through darkness on the day new-born.
Thou comest, like some Bird of Paradise,
    Fluttering its sunny wings so tenderly,
Stirring the rapt soul with thy loveliness,
                 Spirit of Liberty!

Weary Earth hails thy coming ;—With what might
    Rolls the deep tide of being at thy feet!
Its heaving billows panting at the sight
    In bright foam circles—passionate to greet

Thy regal presence—Labor's peerless Queen!
  Restore the Eden of Humanity
Unto the World's sere heart—with joy serene,
                          Celestial Liberty!

Poland awaits thee; Sad, ill-fated land!
  Ah! not extinguished *yet*, its hero flame;
And Hungary, tomb of a martyr band—
  Brave Hungary! glory-gemmed gallant name:—
Old Rome looks up to her Italian sky,
  Her lofty domes outstretched to welcome thee:
Oh, Hearts expand, like flowers when summer's nigh,
                          'Neath thy light, Liberty!

From his high throne proud Jura looks and smiles
  O'er the land hallowed by the name of Tell;
The bright dawn, of which Patriots dreamt erewhiles,
  Will glow in radiance where they bled and fell.
Greece—home of Science, cradle-place of Song,
  Nurse of the Spartan hearts, fearless and free,
Strains her old eyes to view, through turgid Wrong,
                          Thy lost light, Liberty!

The far-off West hath heard a cheering cry,
  And dried her tears amid her sore distress;

Mild Hope went, lark-like, singing up the sky,
   From the dire swamp of Slavery's wilderness ;—
The echoing air bore surges of the song,
   The shackled trembling Captive bent his knee,
For, Christ-like, walking o'er the waves of Wrong,
          He saw thee, Liberty !

Gladness shall thrill throughout the Earth—East, West,
   Shall blend their praise, in one exultant voice ;
Quickly will beat the pulses of the oppressed—
   How will the Slave, long trodden, crushed, rejoice !
The sad Old-World cast off her mourning robes,
   Wave her glad banners proudly o'er the sea,—
Sparkle the New-World's eyes, like Morn's dew-globes,
          In the sun, Liberty !

The muffled music of the Heart's mute strings
   Shall startle Silence at thy magic touch ;
And Heaven-ward waft Elysian melodies
   To the bright throne of Him, who formed thee such.
The exile, Soul regain its palace-home—
   Life's tree long flowerless bloom immortally—
God's thoughts smile upward thro' the bursting gloom,
          Revealing Liberty !

Wrecked hoary Tyranny in dust shall rot:—
That once despotic monarch of the World,—
The power that dealt such cruel blows forgot,
His sword of flame to far oblivion hurled;
Unshackled now the Bondsmen of his wrath,
(Stirring within each spirit, Deity),
Shall write the words " *No more !*" his epitaph,
    By thy light, Liberty !

" *No more* " the powerless man, despised and weak,—
Shall quench the glowing seraph-fire in tears,
Wring the Heart's life-blood, blanch the withered cheek,
And wear the sinews out in servile fears;
No more a crouching drudge in Mammon's mine—
Thy glorious light dawns from Eternity;
He'll rise, the Poor man, *Manly* at thy shrine,
    Goddess of Liberty !

From the dull ashes of the valiant hearts
Who proudly leapt to death through gory seas,
Fresh flowers, a coronal for Truth, upstarts,
Like bursting buds, when Spring-days warm the leas.
Our Father-land shall greater, nobler, rise ;
As, after Winter's sleep, earth's greenery,—
The echoing shout awake the startled skies,
    Hail, Heaven-born Liberty !

57

The clarion voice arouse the slumbering world,
   And re-assure faint drooping Adam's sons,—
Freedom's white banner, o'er the Earth unfurled,
   Proclaims bright Liberty—She comes! She comes!
Plants from the clod up-shoot of Sovereign Truth,
   In the waste places, let them blossom free,—
Your hearts shall summer in eternal Youth,
             Children of Liberty!

Light 'mid the world's dark shadows;—Mightily
   Strike the cold darkling sod; Break Beauty's calm,
Burst into myriad ripples Life's dull sea,
   Attune the silent hills to a sweet psalm;
The resurrection-morn of buried hopes
   Soon through the misty clouds beam gloriously;
Breathe on the dry-bones—Renovate the clay,
             Spirit of Liberty!

THE DEATH OF DAY.

Hush! roving Winds, breathe softly—*Day is dead!*
To wrap him in his shroud, dark solemn Night
Leading back Silence; with slow stealthy tread
Descendeth from her lofty Watch-tower's height.

And all is still—Nature's bright transport fled—
All still, save tremblings faint of forest leaves—
Earth's winsome smiles are flown; for Day is dead, —
All still, save the deep sighs old Ocean heaves.

The thronging Shadows, through the heavenly clime,
Followed by Stars—a train of brilliancy—
Are bearing him away beyond Time's bounds,
To his lone tomb, in far Eternity.

Methinks from flowerets pale, from hoary oaks,
The mournful words, grief-stricken, David's wail,
" Thou'lt not return to me ! "—comes low but clear,
Like dying music, sighed upon the gale.

It was a Sabbath ! God's free day of love !
Who dared, with vice, its purity to stain ?
Whose heart-prayer echoed to the realms above ?
The *day* is past—its *deeds* will yet remain.

Oh, holy hour ! Thought-loving hour sublime !
The Spirit breathes on our rebellious will ;
Each breeze seems Angels' sounding wings through Time,
Lifting our souls to Heaven ; deep, calm, and still !

Yet morn will dawn ;   Waking Earth joyous look—
With smiles forget the yester-morn's bright ray ;
Will *Man* forget?   On the recording Book
The *Angel* noted down, " *The Death of Day.*"

MEMORIES.

Oh! memories of Childhood's friends are twined around my heart ;
Wreathed in a chain whose sparkling links after-years cannot part;—
Sharers of little griefs and joys, all through the chequered day,
Loved thoughts of you—Oblivion's wing can never sweep away !
Companions of my childish games, whose friendship knew no doubt,
Oft have our voices mingled in school-day's merry shout ;
We've wandered the meads together, we've culled the water-flower,—
Heard the wild song-birds in the glen chant from their leafy bower ;
With thoughts pure as the morning dew, and hearts as full of joy
As the singing lark that hymns his praise to God in yon bright sky;—
Much-loved light-hearted school-fellows; Where, oh! where are ye
    now ?
Some in far lands, I ween, and some on ocean's rugged brow ;
Some, ah! *many* in Spirit-land, that realm of lasting light,
Concealed from us by Time's dark veil, and Death's mysterious night!

61

Voices are ringing in my ears, loving hands are clasped in mine,—
Shadows rise before me, the ghosts of olden time !
I'm bounding o'er the smooth green sward, with spirits free and wild,
My comrades shout, and dear old friends hail me once more a child!—
But no, no, it was all a dream! the vision passed away,—
Sorrow and change have been with me, since the bright golden day
When earth, and sea, and sky looked glad, all nature smiled on me,—
The tall old trees in waving woods, and flowerets on the lea ;
The feathered choristers, that seem to feel the joy they give,
All sang, "To live is blessedness, 'tis blessedness to live !"
And *I* could but echo back the song of a happy world like this,
(Childhood's heart leaps with some innate, glad consciousness of
      bliss.)—

The illusion fled : Youth's bright hours came trooping gaily on—
With vague regrets, that ever blend with hopes of the To-come.:
Fluttering Thought said, "Live to what end ? to sweat and toil for
      gold ?—
Or waste a life in useless dreams, wake, find yourself grown old ?"
And Conscience whispered, "Ah ! take heed, or thou wilt starve the
      Soul!"
Alas ! I saw the World forgot, "the *grave* was not life's *goal ;*"
But wandered darkling over Earth, smit with the plague of gold;—
Whose rank pestilential breath breeds Avarice dank and cold ;

Freezing the fountains of the heart, hard as drear Autumn's bier,
Binding, with adamantine chains, the Angel-Stranger here.

. . . .

Nature yet speaks; Lo! Night hath thrown her mantle over Earth;—
Loud Trade is hushed, and Silence creeps into the halls of Mirth:
While seated on her throne, Night tells the universe of stars,
Of awful things which she hath seen—of Wrong, of Pride, of Wars!
Uncrowned she sitteth now, robed in a sable garb of woe,
And speaketh of a world where Sin hath hidden Truth's bright
    glow;—
The pale Moon came forth to listen; and all the orbs above
Heard Night say, "Your poor Sister Earth hath lost the name of
    Love:"
Her children, full of hate, crush and jar against each other—
There's little of that feeling left which says, "I'll help thee, brother!"
Heaven oped her trembling eye-lids, and looked down where old
    Earth slept;
Night said, "Oh! Truth and Love may call, she'll list not,"—here
    Night wept.

. . . .

To me trees clap their leafy hands, and wave in joy no more;
Honeysuckled hedgerows are not so fragrant as of yore;
Why, why? I ask this heart of mine, the sunbeams are as bright,
Though clouds oft gather o'er the sky, they still are fringed with
    light;—

Oh ! wreath of Memory still fair, still beautiful thou art,
Thou shalt not wither like pale flowers, that bloom but to depart ;
My early friends, Thought's mirror still reflects ye as ye *were*,
Careless as the wild mountain breeze, free as the mountain air !
But much I fear me that on each, erst candid, cloudless brow,
The World hath set its signet-mark—distrust, doubt, cold scorn,
    now ;—
The lights of smiles dance o'er those eyes, like wild-fire o'er a bog,
Truth beams but dimly, as a star obscured by mist and fog ;—
Then let me cherish memories, all glad, and fresh, and bright,
As waves of laughing streams that dance in summer's noon-day
    light.

. . . .

Come, Brothers, Sisters, trim anew Love's lamp, ere its last ray
Goes out on Earth, and we have slept the dreamless sleep in Clay ;—
That which aspires grows brighter,—Smoke poured forth of murky
    hue,
Rises clear and silv'ry in air, then melts into the blue ;—
Thus, Brothers, let the Earth-stained soul soar from the clammy sod,
Ascend, still brighten, till at last it meets its glorious God !
Wipe the gold-dust from our blinded eyes, and, like eaglets to the sun,
With steadfast gaze, soar upwards, till Heaven's blissful shores are
    won !

THE CHILD'S GRAVE.

LOUD roared the ruthless tempest-king
   Across the dreary wold,
While from the lonely ivied tower
   The solemn death-knell tolled :—
Where darkly o'er the coffined dead
   The old yew, like a pall,
Its sombre branches widely spreads,
   Close to the church-yard wall—
The little one was laid to rest
   In slumber long and deep—
The burial train dispersed ; to homes
   Of joy went some, and some to weep ;
Little Willie, merry play-fellow !
   They left amid the graves ;

To sleep where winds loud wailings blend
   With music of the waves ;—

   .   .   .   .

Sorrow that chills the heart's warm blood
   And drains tear-fountains dry ;—
Wild Woe, that blows our hopes to shreds,
   Like clouds through Autumn's sky ;—
Death's frost, that nips the tender bud,
   And spares the shiv'ring leaf ;
Ye are the sternest foes of Man,
   Chequering Life with grief !—
Oh ! little Willie, beauteous child,
   The fondest, youngest born,
We listen for thy silvery voice,
   Noon, eve, and dewy morn—
We are waiting for thee, Willie,
   And wilt thou never come ?
Like broken harp-strings, must our hearts
   For ever more be dumb ?—

   .   .   .   .

The snow had left the mountain side
   To its bright robe of green ;—
And here and there a speck of blue
   Through the grey clouds was seen—

It was the time when copse and glade,
  And sunny slanting hills,
Echo the prattling babble of
  A thousand tiny rills;—
We stood beside the little grave,
  And wept, and called the child—
The sunshine gleaming through the yew's
  Broad arms, gleamed on, and smiled—
Winds sweeping through the winking boughs,
  Shaking away each tear—
Like the Angel at the grave of old,
  Whispered, "He is not here!"—

.   .   .   .

There was a glory everywhere:—
  Hawthorn trees were budding,
And all the giant forest oaks
  Leafy garlands weaving,
To crown the sweet young virgin May,
  When from eastern bowers
The sunny Hours would lead her; Earth
  Strew her pathway with flowers;
And golden king-cups on the leas
  The merry fairies find,

And spangled threads of gossamer
   Wave in the gentle wind.

.   .   .   .

Once more from Afric's sunny clime
   Returned the wandering swallow ;—
Resounding through the dell was heard
   The cuckoo's music mellow :
The meadow-plains were wildly gay,
   Fresh touched with Flora's wand—
And a blissful living Eden,
   Seemed all the smiling land—
And on our little Willie's grave
   The lily's tiny bells,
And daisy, with its crimson crown,
   Waved in the zephyr's swells;
The daisy shook its little head,
   And from the lily's breath
A voice arose, or seemed to rise,
   " O ye of little faith !"

THE BEAUTIFUL.

A SPIRIT wanders through the world,
   Lingering 'mid the Hours,
Wafting light odours, as of old,
   In Paradise' green bowers;—
With the same beaming smile that shone
   On morn of Nature's birth;
'Tis the spirit of the Beautiful,
   Bright Angel of the Earth!

It hovers o'er the hillside slopes,
   It wakes the streams to song,
And leads the Nymphs and Muses
   The forest-shades among;
The floating cloud o'er summer's sky
   To silvery shreds is riven,

And the Spirit passes softly,
    As a still dream of Heaven.

Even now I mark its presence—
    Hark! the wood-songsters sing;
Mountain-echoes start, and listen
    To the merry laugh of Spring;
As with light footsteps, fairy-like,
    She treads the gloomy hours,
And culls from Winter's cold turf-tomb
    A coronal of flowers!

The proud leaf bursts the yielding stem;
    The rose and hawthorn bloom;
Old ocean on its rocky beach
    Murmurs a softer tune;
Blithesome children come to gather
    Flowers, "Stars" of the soil;
And with joy bound homeward, laden
    With the fast-fading spoil;—

Man—the rich—may gaze in rapture,
    Type of all loveliness!
At thy ever-varying grandeur,
    Forgetful of distress;

Of all gloom and sorrow heedless,
  'Mid the sunshine and the light,
He revels in the Beautiful,
  And basks in pure delight;—

But Man, the pallid toiler—
  In City dark and dun,
Where smoke shuts out the cooling breeze,
  Obscures God's brilliant Sun;—
As ceaseless toiling morn and eve,
  The life-tide in his veins,
Pants for the Beautiful to burst
  Dull Labor's weary chains—

The Sabbath dawns—"the poor man's day "
  With glad heart forth he hies
Where Nature's hoary turrets tower
  To the deep azure skies;
Where gurgling rills wind to the main,
  Where woods are waving free,
God of the Beautiful! he comes,
  T' adore and worship Thee.

The purple-tinted clouds of eve—
  Soft twilight's misty hue,—

71

Night, when the sparkling starry orbs
  Peep through the spotless blue ;
Earth's glories, countless as the shells
  On ocean's pebbly strand—
All, all display thy magic power,
  The Beautiful, the Grand !

NEW YEAR'S DAY IN DREAMLAND.

LIKE mournful watchers round the bed
　　Of one whose life wanes fast ;
The tall old trees stood mute and still—
　　Breath-like, the old year passed—
Amid the silence of the night,
　　When winds had sobbed their last.

With wreaths of sparkling frost-work crowned,
　　Came in the crisping morn ;—
Ere the star-lamps paled in the sky,
　　Another year was born ;
Joys budded in the heart, like May's
　　Rich blossoms on the thorn.

73

Oh, with what ecstasy we hailed
    This happy New Year's day!
Beside our hearth Pain should not come,
    And Sorrow dared not stay—
It was the time our absent one
    Would come from far away !—

Sounds floated through the misty air,
    Sweet sounds of merry chimes—
Stole softly on my listening ear,
    Like long-forgotten rhymes,
By unseen mystic voices sung—
    Murmurs of other times.

Morn waxed to noon, and noon to eve—
    Pale eve, so calm and fair—
Up the dim valley twilight came,
    And thou wert with me there—
Thou, with thy speaking sea-blue eyes,
    And sunny clustering hair :—

As ivy-plant enrooted in
    Some dark and crumbling pile,
Expands its leaves unto the light,
    And greener grows the while,—

I turned to thee, and sunned me in
    The radiance of thy smile.

Thine eyes, so full of love and faith,
    Beamed on me as of yore ;
And thou wouldst rest thyself, and stay,
    And leave us never more !—
Alas ! such rest the weary wave
    Finds on the sandy shore :—

'Twas Dream-land ; Time and Space are lost,
    Those realms own not their sway,—
The Eden-gates of Sleep were closed,
    And ah ! I must not stay—
Reality's stern New-Year's morn
    Rose, misty, cold, and grey.

Like Penitence, with bitter tears,
    Bewailing mis-spent hours ;—
A cloud which darkened all the sky,
    By fits wept drizzling showers ;
Wild gusts of wind, like angry ghosts,
    Shrieked through the ruined bowers ;

And thou wert,—where? 'mid fragrant groves
   Of a far stranger-land—
Will no kind greeting reach thee there,
   Nor clasp of friendly hand?—
And shall we never welcome thee
   Back to our household band?—

Perchance, dear friend, 'neath foreign skies'
   Calm and unclouded dome;
Through Night's deep hush, the unsleeping Soul,
   Mem'ry, and Fancy roam
On dreamy wings to this old land,
   And New-Year's day at home!

THE MERRY HEART OF CHILDHOOD.

OH ! what a blissful thing
  Is the merry heart of Childhood ;—
Free as the lightsome breeze
  Playing in leafy wildwood—
Glad as the leaping waves
  'Mong the tangled sea-weed locks—
Wild as the fearless bird
  That nestles amid the rocks.

Oh ! what a sunny thing
  Is bright Childhood's love-lit smile !
Bright as sun-rays that gild
  The banks of some beauteous isle,—

Bright as the Visions of sleep
    That hallow infant eyes;
Bright as the blooming flowers,
    Or the dews of Paradise ;—

Oh, what a joyous thing
    Is Childhood's heartsome laughter!
Brimful of music sweet,
    As silv'ry rippling water ;—
List to the ringing tones—
    Ringing like clear-sounding bells,
Elysian carolling bliss,
    Through their rising cadence swells.

And oh! in Childhood's day
    With what thoughts the soul is stirred!
What mystic voices speak,
    In rapturous tones,—unheard
Save by the infant-soul—
    Of old primeval Eden—
Thoughts come softly whispering
    Of God, of Home, of Heaven!

Why should that heart grow sere ?
    Why should fade that sunny smile ?

Why die with the Years, the laugh?
Oh! why should the World beguile?
While the soul, with weary wings,
    Child, loves not joys of thine,—
The erring spirit sees
    The gathering shades of Time.

Oh! but to feel again
    Like yon gladsome child at play,—
Watching the restless birds,
    Restless and gay as they—
To think pure Childhood's thoughts,
    To feel its spirit-glow;
Ere, heaving parting sighs,
    I fade from the life below!

CHRISTMAS IS COMING!

CHRISTMAS is coming! and beauteous as morning
  Brightly to Dreamer's wan eye-lids unfolden;
It comes to the free heart; The glorious adorning,
  Crown of the merry old year, glad and golden;
Then weave we the green box, and twine up the holly;
  Once more its red berries hang over the hearth;
Dear homely old custom, deride not as folly—
  Old Christmas is coming, with joyance and mirth!

Ay, "Christmas is coming!" When last it was uttered
  Shrill war trumpets woke the black eagle's fierce cry—
Thund'ring destruction, the hoarse cannon muttered;
  Arms clanking, swords clashing, rang thro' the far sky;—

While sons, friends, and brothers, Death's dark tide were
    breasting—
Who then could be merry? while gallant ones bled!
God be thanked! the stained sword in its scabbard is resting,
    Peace smiles, now grass waves o'er the graves of the dead.

Old Christmas is coming! But dimly the fire-light,
    Fantastic and ghostlike plays on the wall,
In full many a home, where faded the love-light,
    Grim Sorrow broods over the hearth like a pall;
The sweet-toned Bird of Happiness never-more sings;
    Sighs from soul-depths are heaved, and bitter tears shed,—
Young Gladness hath flown, and Peace folded its wings;
    Ah! though Christmas is coming, it brings not the Dead!

Bleak Christmas is coming! Cold hooded and darkling,
    The long hours creep slowly where stricken ones pine;—
Gay Christmas is coming! and bright eyes are sparkling
    Where Wit peals its jokes o'er the clear ruby wine;
There Childhood is happy; Youth joyous, and quicker,
    Through the Aged one's blue veins, now courses the blood;—
While the Children of Poverty listen, and wonder,
    Through the dull wintry night, if there *can* be a God!

Old Christmas is coming! Forget not the homeless,
  'Mid music and pleasure, and revelry's din ;—
Those wandering ones, lonely, life-weary, and loveless,
  Who, Arab-like, traverse the desert of Sin ;—
While Wealth's board is creaking, say, say, shall these perish?
  Shall Hunger's cold fingers their life-fountain freeze ?
Forget not the homeless, the fainting one cherish ;
  Oh, Christmas is coming ; but sadly to these !

Blithe Christmas is coming ! May joy in our bosoms
  Bid Care's brooding shadows, and dim fears depart—
And hopes, glad and pure, wave in bright cluster blossoms,
  Like snow-drops of winter, 'neath sunshine of heart—
Oh, joy ! though the Old Year is waning and dying,
  And outside, the angry Winds drive the cold sleet,
Warm Friendship shall live, the World's rude blasts defying—
  Old Christmas is coming ! And loved ones shall meet.

1856.

THIS IS DEATH.

CLOSE the dim glassy eyes,
They will beam on us no more !
The slightly-parted lips still wear the smile they wore
When rich carnation'd with the hue of Life ;—
But from a world, where storms are rife,
God bade the spirit soar
Away beyond the skies ;—

No more the light warm breath
Shall, surge-like, come and go !
What wouldst thou to thy much-loved Sister speak ?
    Bend low,
Whisper thy words, or thunder in her ear ;
Ah ! motionless, she will not hear—

Deaf, deaf to friend or foe,
Sorrow or joy beneath!—

What mortal tongue shall say,
What course upon its flight
The unfettered Spirit took? Through realms of night,
By flaming Seraphs led upon its way,
And strains angelic—Did it leave its Clay
Welcomed by smiles of Light,
To bliss and endless Day?—

Silent; nor sign nor word
Hath reached us from that land;—
Nor of the myriads, countless as the sand,
That left Time's shores for the Eternity,
Hath one returned, to tell the mystery
Of Doom—or of that band
In presence of the Lord:

This is a rest that waits
Th' Archangel's note—A sleep
All dreamless—Storms may sweep
Creation's depths; but this they cannot wake;—
Nor Earth, although her mountains quake,
Rouse; till the last dawn peep
Through Heaven's bright gates!

Freedom from pain and grief ;—
All crosses—sorrows cease ;
Nor ever dare to mar this last, calm peace !
The Monarch of Fears ! King of the world beneath
Reigns here—tread softly—this is *Death !*—
A Vict'ry—the release
Endless—the struggle brief !

We too hasten onward :—
Life, that like streamlet mild
Rippled at first, at length will roar, a torrent wild,
And bear us swiftly on its foaming wave,
Until we sink in the deep caverned Grave ;—
After Time's storms—the tomb be rest !
And the Soul's unknown flight
Be God-ward—Heavenward !

MOVE ON.

THE murm'ring river hastens on,
  Seeking its ocean-home;
Tides, ever-surging, ebb and flow,
  Winds o'er earth ceaseless roam;
Winter scarce leaves our sea-girt isle,
  Ere the life-giving Sun
Beholds the smiling infant Spring ;—
  Untiring—*All* move on.

Move on ! Fair Summer quickly flies—
  Autumn, with sere decay
Spreads over all—Night soon enshrouds
  The longest, brightest day.

86

Along the wondrous chain of Time—
    Links added one by one,
A bridge from Earth to Spirit-land,
    We soon must pass—Move on !

The mighty mission of the Soul—
    Oh, were it understood !
Then would our dreary world appear
    Like Paradise the Good.
Blest be the man! that can uplift
    The plodding weary one
From earth—point out his heritage—
    Shall *we* not try—Move on !

Friends, let us the blinding gold-dust
    Wipe from our care-worn eyes ;—
Waken the Soul from trance-like sleep,
    For much within us lies ;
The highest rank Earth can bestow,
    Fame, Glory, to be won,
Is *far* beneath the *lofty* Soul—
    Earth is not *Home*—Move on !

The God-like, King-souls of all Time
    Hover above us *now*,

Beckoning us on to twine a wreath
  For Freedom's noble brow :
The eternal flashing star of Truth,
  O'er darkling Earth shines on—
Bidding us follow in the track
  Of mighty spirits gone !

Ah ! from afar I see the dawn
  Of a bright glorious time,
When earth shall smile in radiance
  Unmarr'd by sin and crime ;
When Strife and Hate shall pass away,
  Like mists 'fore morning's sun ;
The Immortal Principle of Right
  Rule over all—Move on !

For that good time the clarion cry
  Calls us, " Uprouse ye, then !"
With *lightning-thoughts*, with *thunder-deeds*,
  Labor with Press and Pen
Untiringly—there's rest in Heaven
  When the bright goal is won :
The watch-word of the Brave and Free
  Should ever be—" Move on !"

THE EDEN OF LOVE.

WHERE is Love's Eden? On what spot of Earth?—
In the East, the bright land of morning's birth?
Or the golden climes, where the setting sun
Sinks to rest when his brilliant goal is won?—
Is it far away in some happy isle,
Where roses of summer for ever smile—
'Neath the soothing shade of the lofty palm,
Where breezes blow laden with sweetest balm,
Where the glad leaping billows with murmur deep
Are lulling the calm leafy shores to sleep?—
Ay, all may be bright, 'neath that azure dome,
Yet *that* is not Eden—Love's blessed home!

The lark soareth high in the morning air,
Far, far 'bove the snowy-white cloudlets fair;

He is singing now, lost to mortal view,
In some nook in yon heavenly arch of blue—
Scattering musical snatches of bliss,
O'er climes a thousand times fairer than this;
But, list! for the sweet sounds are floating near,
'Tis the bird of the sky, hastening here;
He descendeth now to his grassy nest,
To his birdie blithe—loveliest and best;
And the lark returneth e'en from above,
For *this* is his *home—his* Eden of Love!

Love calls *no* clime his own,—To him as bright
Dark Laplandian hills, as Persian vales light,
If there a warm heart vibrates to his own,
He heedeth not—feeleth not, in what zone;—
He may rove o'er the wide, far fields of life,
Be lost awhile, 'mid Trade's turmoil and strife;
'Mid the crash and the clanking of War—Be hurled
O'er the waves of the ever-surging world;—
But see the all-potent magical art
Of the pure ark of home! To *one* loved heart
He returneth, like Noah's wing-weary dove;
For the *heart* is the home, and the *Eden* of Love.

LIGHT IN DARKNESS.

"Sorrow not as those without hope."

SORROW not overmuch, Children of grief
   However darksome, and however sore,—
Though Time bring no kind cordial of relief,
   If gentle Hope be thine—Hope silvers o'er,
With holy light, the flooding tide of Woe ;—
   And as some troubled river's rapid waves
Reflect a radiance from the crescent bow
     Of Night's fair Queen—though 'round the storm-
     wind raves,
And sullen Desolation resteth there,
   Throned in deep gloom—Yet Ether's fields afar

Bear on their azure front a happy star,
  That gleaming on the ebon crest of Night,
Tells doubting, cloud-veiled worlds, their " God is
    Light !"

BEAUTY AND JOY.

Ye linger not here on this earth, I ween ;
But ye garnish woods with silvery sheen,
And ye light up the wolds with a rosy glow,
When sunbeams glisten o'er Winter's snow ;—

Yet while Eve decks her tresses with pearly dew,
Joy is waving his hand in a fond adieu ;
And Beauty is gone on a western cloud,
While Change foldeth hills in a misty shroud.

Ah ! Beauty and Joy, far in leafy bowers
Shall we seek you ; amidst the sweets of flowers ?
Or in tangled wild-woods of forest shades—
Or walking the valley's pleasant glades ?

Or 'mong sea-weed, graceful as Nereid's hair,
With pinky shells, 'broidering your pleasant lair,
On some lone rocky pyramid, rising free
From the dancing waves of a summer sea ?

Beauty and Joy, why haste ye away ?
Like Iris' hues of an April day ;
Or meteor's gleam, ye glance o'er the heart,
And our faint eyes but see your forms depart.

Ye *have* a home too, Twin-spirits bright—
A soaring lark far from mortal sight
I thought had found it ; so blithe his lay,
As he winged his flight on his trackless way—

So full of joyance, greeting this morn ;—
But, ah me ! he returned to wail forlorn,
Back to earth 'mong the tasselled corn
O'er a nest despoiled, and young ones torn !

Thus ever here,—All must soon forego
The gay notes of joy, for sounds of woe ;
Yet, from Cotter's hut to Monarch's hall,
'Bove the world's din, somewhere, Joy singeth to all.

94

And ye have a *home*—oh, ye *have* a home!
Where sighing and sorrow can nevermore come :
Blest bearers of hope, unto mortals given,
Of the glory and light of Eternity's Heaven!

THE SUN 'S BEHIND THE HILLS.

THOUGH frost may bind in icy chains
  The surface of the stream—
The restless under-current still
  Ripples with sparkling gleam :
                  Hope on !

Again shall glow the spring-tide light,
  Whose fragrance balm distils ;
Winter will quickly pass ; cheer up,
  The Sun 's behind the hills !—

Let not despair o'ershadow thee ;
  Look at the gladsome lark,
He, when the glorious evening fades,
  Still through the frowning dark
                  Hopes on,

And ere the sleeping Dawn awakes,
Ether's wide plain he fills
With ringing carols; telling Earth
" The Sun 's behind the hills !"

Oh, never yet was lonesome night
But some meek kindly star,
The Angel Hope's bright messenger,
Shone silvery afar;

Hope on !

Though slow and long the dismal watch,
Though fraught with countless ills;
Cheer up ! 'Twill all be over soon,
The Sun 's behind the hills !

A FAREWELL TO THE YEAR 1857.

SILENCE rests on earth below;
The midnight winds are sighing low—
And we will out and see thee go—
    Watch thy departure!

Brave old Year! Loved heretofore—
Another comes; thy course is o'er—
And oh! we fear, heart-sick and sore,
    That unknown future!

For-ever, take we leave of thee?
Or, somewhere in Eternity,
Wilt thou—thoughts, feelings, actions—*be*
    Sweet Mem'ry's essence?

And disencumbered of the clay—
All worldly woes long past away—
We'll meet thee in the realm of Day,
  A living presence?

Fading Year! we hailed thy birth
With gladsome hearts and happy mirth—
Yes, and with thee in Sorrow's dearth,
  When fell Griefs banish

Light from bright eyes;—We've stood beside
The bed of Sickness, there descried
Friends struggling in Death's swelling tide,
  Swept down and vanish!

We *may* hail many a Winter's rime;
Spring, Summer's roses, Christmas chime—
But " fifty-seven " (thy name in time)
  Will yet be dearer,

Whene'er by chance it strikes my ear,
Yes, though it start the sudden tear—
Than to the leafless forests drear
  (Pale Autumn's cheerer)

The red-breast's gay and sprightly note—
Gurgles of brooklets learnt by rote,
Stirring amid that tiny throat
  A faint remembrance

Of rosy morns, and purple eves,—
Of flower-clad meads and nodding leaves—
With harvest-homes, and golden sheaves,
  And old acquaintance!—

But ah ! 'tis twelve—and sad and slow
The old clock warns us ;—to and fro
Trees wave good-bye to " long-ago,"
  The dismal death-knell

Startles the midnight's frosty air,—
Whilst thou, past the last starry stair,
Old Year, ascendest up, up there—
  Farewell, a long farewell!

THE CHRISTIAN'S DEATH.

"How wilt thou do in the swellings of Jordan?"
HOLY WRIT.

HE stood upon the confines of a world
Of care, and doubt, and pain—O'er the half Earth
Lay spread the sable covering of deep Night—
The *Wind*—Spirit's sublimest emblem—roared
Through the woods; hoarsely and furiously
Swept o'er the plain, where huddled lay in flocks
The timid sheep, and frighted droves of kine—
And speeding up the lone deserted road,
Whirled the wild hedge-row blossoms from their stems,—
Rattling with fitful gusts old crazy huts,
Whose wattled chimneys long had borne the brunt

Of savage storms—Wild wind!—away it went,
Stirring to mimic waves the stagnant pools;
Rounding the hill, careering through the dale,
Up the green shady lane 'tween hazel trees;—
Muttering fiercely at the Poor man's door.

'Twas midnight, girt around with frowning clouds—
With scarce a star to cheer the saddened earth.

A narrow casement shows a light within,
A feeble taper struggles to chase back
The looming darkness of the humble room,
Where, on a lowly pallet stretched, Disease
Worked hard to break the precious silver cord
Of Life's warm fountain.—

Deep was the valley, shadowed o'er
By fearful darkness—Silent, deep, and dark;
But hark! there is a rushing sound
Of waters, dashing, surging, somewhere down
The dismal cold ravine—Listen! that vale
Is called "The valley of the shadow, *Death*,"
And that loud river there "The swelling Jordan."

And he, a human spirit, must pass down
The awful vale, pass through the gate of Fears,

And lo ! he falters not ; but with a smile,
A happy smile upon his pallid face,
A heavenly brightness lighting up his eyes—
He casts a farewell glance on earthly things:—

And he hath passed adown the murky path ;
Louder and louder in his ear resounds
The rushing waters ;—Still the shadow broods
And circles all around—but as his feet
Touch the deep river's edge, a glorious light
Enkindles from beyond—*Now* he can see
The foaming waves, and, with his rod of Faith,
Feel the unfailing rock beneath—Brighter
Grows the Light—glows—broadens into Day—
As blissful echoes of Angelic strains
Deafen the roar of waters !

And he hath passed into a land of light—
Passed through where mortal dare not follow.

'Twas Morn on Earth ; and perfumes, sweet
As spice of Araby, were breathed around—
The silent sighs of myriad flowery plants
Made odorous the air of tender Spring ;—
And sparkling dew-drops were exhaled to Heaven,

To glitter there in cloudlets snowy white,
Or rich-hued rainbows beautiful.

'Twas Morning in the busy bustling world—
That tiny drop of great Humanity;
The poor old man; the Christian Kingly Soul—
Was lost to earth; and neighbours gathered round
The Clay, and in full-hearted sympathy
Cried, "Oh! our Friend, our Brother! Ah,
And did he die!"

THE WORLD'S FAVORITE.

"A poor wise man is like a sacred book that's never read."
DECKER.

IN this hard slippery world
It is not he—the kind good man, whose Soul
Is lit with wisdom from the heavenly heights,—
Who lends a helping hand unto the weak,
And, like the good Samaritan, pours oil
Into the wounds of the unfortunate—
That's lauded most—The Worldling vieweth such
With the same admiration as some star
He sees there twinkling in the blue remote ;—
" All well to look upon, and bright," saith he,
" But then for use—stars,—Stars are too nigh heav'n,
So give *me* gaslight "—Nor yet is it he,

Who creeps unnoticed, calmly, meekly on
With sweetest smile serenely down to Death ;—
But he—the cat-like, velvety-paced man,
Who climbs and climbs—and falls—and climbs again—
Clinging to anything within his reach,—
And though he fall, falls ever on his feet—
Still ready for another start,—For *him*
There's nought too low, or long, or tedious—
Cat-like ; yes, the analogy is clear—
A long dark night of unremitting watch
Tires not his patience,—with a mouse in view—
Many-lived Man !—Though battered oft—ne'er killed,
Till the last stern strong Tyrant drags away,—
Ere he hath time with equity to deal
Unto his anxious heirs his weight of wealth—
And warn them not like thankless dogs to snarl,
And let Law cudgel them to peace again ;—
Death drags away the Rich, *Successful* man ;
The Idol of this happy, gifted age.

AUTUMN.

I.

The Autumn mists hang over wood and wold;—
　Songsters seem dreaming in the dripping brake;
While Morning ushers in, through damp and cold,
　Day's half-veiled chariot; O'er the glassy lake
The listless flags droop wearily;—Old orchard trees
　Are gay, while peeping through the mottled leaves
Are red-cheeked apples, waiting for a breeze;—
　Plenty reigns everywhere—The golden sheaves
Safe garnered—Autumn laughs, while round his head
The Hours twine poppy-flowers, white and red.

II.

I turn to watch a swallow leave its nest—
Its mud-built home beneath our granary eaves,
It grieves to bid adieu—but on the crest
Of yon dark sky it reads of storms ; dead leaves
Rustle a tale of forests tempest-tost—
Of wintry days, with blackening clouds and rain ;
Of hail, and snows, of sleet, and biting frost—
Of blank decay—famine, and woe, and pain !

III.

Ha ! little swallow, I must see thee go—
Thou leav'st our humble homestead, for a clime
More sunny than these lands, where winds oft blow :
Thou seek'st the land of myrtle, palm, and lime,—
But many are the dangers of the deep—
Wild Æolus rough, may there in madness rave ;—
Ocean is terrible, e'en when lulled to sleep ;—
How dreadful then in fury ?—Many a cave
Of gloom and death it hath—Thy cry of pain,
Or faint sweet tone of joy, when far away
Will ne'er be heard—On the deep-sounding main
The petrel's shriek, or sea-mew's note when Day

Breaks from the East, will echo on thy track ;—
   But thou art flown ! adieu, poor Bird !
   Some morn when Spring's sweet music 's heard,
And blossoms scent the gale, I'll hope to see thee back.

EVENING.

BEAUTIFUL is Eve!
Fairer than Noon or Night;
She cometh from the burnished halls
      Where the sun sinks to rest ;
Her footsteps leave a purple glow
      Upon the feath'ry clouds ;—
Beautiful is Eve!

Beautiful is Eve!
The patriarchal hills
Smile as they watch, through rain-bowed mists,
      Her queenly form ascend the pathless skies ;
Smiling benignly on the ebon King,

Who lays his bright star-treasures at her feet,
And calls the young Moon from her azure couch,
　　To light her to her rest in heaven ;—

　　After Life's weary day
Tranquillity like this,
Spread o'er the even of my years,
　　When Night is creeping on !
Herald a dawn more glorious—
　　And leave a holy glow,
　　Beautiful as Eve !

THE WILD, WILD WAVES.

Oh, a gladsome song, the wild, wild waves
  Chant to the glistening shore,
As they gaily dance from their ocean caves
  While the sunlight flashes o'er ;—

They have laughed round many a green-robed isle;
  And grey rock where sea-weed grew—
Whispered their joy to each coral reef
  That rose from the waste of blue ;—

They have mingled those tones, for the song is old,
  With sounds of each onward Age
Hast'ning, ere Death's clouds o'er it rolled,
  To the goal of its pilgrimage—

Years—a thousand past, its cadence clear
    Was heard by the hosts of Time;
Still will it strike on the Future's ear,
    When the dust has deafened mine!

In the sun the restless billows play,—
    And leap from their ocean lair—
Away they speed on their joyous way,
    Tossing sparkling spray in the air!—

But a wailing strain, the wild, wild waves
    Chant to the listening shore,
As echoes shriek from their rocky caves,
    And the sullen storm-winds roar;—

The heart-felt prayer of the sailor-lad,
    As he clings to the sea-washed deck;—
With cries of the drowning one; and sad
    Deep groans from the shattered wreck;

Half stifled moans, and many a sigh—
    With some weakened swimmer's gasp,
As he faints, he faints though shore is nigh,
    He sinks in the ocean's grasp!

All seem to blend in the woful dirge,
   The wild waves wail on the strand;
With loud shouts and songs the dashing surge
   Hath borne from some distant land;—

Yet, a glad, glad strain the mimic waves
   Bear to the summer light;
As though they wist not of myriad graves
   Deep fathoms below in night!

ODE TO SLEEP

COME, Somnus; come, thou mighty god,
And bear me on the smooth bright road
Which leads to the enchanted palaces
Where Morpheus reigns, with all his fallacies ;—
Where the World's friendship is a firm-wrought link,
Which from cold Poverty doth never shrink ;—
Where Gold is not omnipotent—where Life
With generous acts and kindnesses is rife—
Where favors do not burn like living embers,
The donor's glance shows ever *he* remembers—
Where *Might*, with shaggy eye-brows, cannot frown
The *Right* to black annihilation down—
Where man forgets deceit; and woman vanity ;—
Where piety and " muscular Christianity"

Are one—Bring poppy-buds, and let me slake
My thirst a moment at the Lethean lake :—
Then Morpheus kind, come meet me on the road
To thy enchanted and grotesque abode,
Where Fancy dwells, amid thy train of fallacies,
Thy Queen supreme in rich fantastic palaces.

STORM AND CALM.

ALL through the livelong night
The lightning flashes bright,
Like winkings of an eye of fire, shot o'er the frowning sky;—
Quivered athwart the gloom,
While many an angry boom
Rolled thundering from the grand artillery on high :—
The stricken earth beneath,
Like a child, with stifled breath,
That trembling fears to meet an angry father's frown,
Scarce stirs her forest trees,
While pattering through the leaves
In heavy showers the rain-drops hurriedly roll down—
At the strange light watch-dogs howl—
From yon hollow tree the owl

Hoots shrilly out; The frightened kine start lowing from
    their sleep,—
        While echoes from dark caves
        Waken tranquil waves,
And lo! they foam and dash along the midnight deep!

        Swiftly the thunder car
        Pursues its course; now far
In distance dies the sound,—Dark clouds move on their way,
        But winds in angry strife
        Rise, and the air is rife
With sighs, and moans, and spirit-wails, and ere the break
    of day
        Many, many a gallant bark,
        Far on the billows dark
Floats in broken spars and splinters,—and oh! beneath the
    wave,
        Many a noble head is laid—
        Many fond hearts' beatings staid,—
The loved and loving tossed in a cold unquiet grave;—
        And the cheering morning sun,
        O'er the dreadful havoc done,
Spreads silvery beams of light to gild the dismal scene;—

The winds are hushed to rest,
Old Ocean's panting breast
Bears but the shattered wrecks to show where man hath been!

And calm, calm, calm
Rises morning, with its balm
Of perfumed flowers, and shrubs, and pearly drops of dew ;
The bees with merry hum
To their honied labour come,
And all is gay and bright, as though earth were glad and new.
Scarce a trace remains of night,
With its terrors and affright,—
While song-birds chant their matin hymn on every budding
thorn ;—
Thus, Life's loud thunders o'er,
The surges on Time's shore
Shall still their restless beatings, on a glorious happy morn—
And the calm unclouded sky
Of the blissful heaven on high
Be hailed by Souls immortal, to lasting glory borne,—
When earth, and care, and pain,
Its tempests, storms, and rain—
Shall be changed for climes where flowers bloom for aye, and
bear no thorn.

THE BRAVE LIVE ON.

WEALTH often taketh wings and flieth far away,
And fluttering gaudy butterflies, the insects of a day—
Those flatterers, called friends, with summer flowers are gone,
And "the coward sneaks to death,—the brave lives on !"

Fell Disappointment cometh, like leaves before the blast,
Loved hopes, and schemes, and plans are whirled into the
    past,—
While the future stretcheth gloomily ; a sea without a sun,
" The coward sneaks to death,—the brave lives on !"

All along the dreary dark—wild Ruin and pale Fear
Awe the poor heart that vainly lists for tones it cannot hear,—
For kind voices that might whisper hope have passed him
    one by one,—
And " the coward sneaks to death,—the brave lives on,"

At the humble door stand waiting, with faces grim and bold,
Those weird sisters two—Hunger and pallid Cold :—
And the palsied heart grows still at thought of what they've
   done;
Then " the coward sneaks to death—the brave lives on !"

Crushed Poverty may point from weary years of toil,
And show the wicked reveller amid his corn and oil,
While icy-handed, blank Despair graspeth pale Misery's son,
" The coward sneaks to death,—the brave lives on !"

Though with wings swift as an eagle's, when he eyes the
   god of Day,—
Wealth bear honor, fame, and friends far from his reach
   away,—
Ruin and Want affright—the victory may be won,
For God is with the brave,—he labors, and lives on !

BLIGHTED.

'Twas Winter,—
Softly and silently the feathery
Snow-flakes fell ; as if some spirit bade them
Forth with noiseless wing ;—Earth bared her wrinkled
Brow in reverence ; the grey old trees bowed
Low their ancient heads in grave humility ;
And holy silence reigned o'er all around ;—

In that cold chilly time,
A flower, a fragile flower of a pale
Pinky hue, half hidden in the snow-drift,
Vainly strove to uplift its tiny head
Above the ground ; the timid snow-drop weak,
And hardy crocus braved the icy breath ;
And nestled closer in their milk-white garb ;—

122

But that sweet bud, in uncongenial ground,
Shrunk from the bitter blast—'Twas a rare plant!
Had it been fed with Summer's gentle dew,
Cheered by warm sun-beams and soft zephyrs mild,
It now had blossomed fair, and breathed its
Fragrant perfume over all around.

      A human bud of promise bright,—
Born in the cold bleak clime of Poverty;
Breathing the wintry atmosphere of Want,
Uprose amid a hard and barren world—
A rare exotic from some happy land,
A precious seed it seemed, dropped from the hand
Of radiant Angel on its homeward flight;—
Like plant which meets the Seaman's wond'ring eye,
Up-springing on a lone and rugged rock
Amid the wild waste of a heaving sea—
It rose all pure, unsullied by the gloom,
The murky gloom around, with scarce a trace
Of the dark weary Earth it journeyed through,—
It grew with music ever echoing
Around, the sweet-toned music of its *home*,—
The sullen tempest-roar of crime swept by,
And other sounds save those of wickedness

And misery, were ne'er, or seldom heard ;—
It rose a glorious thing, although unsunned
By smiles of Fortune, or of dazzling Wealth ;
Encircled with a halo from above,
Brave in the alien land, its beauteous head
It lifted high, and through the dismal clouds
Saw kindred forms serenely smiling there ;—
And like those flowerets gazing at the sun,
That ever as they gaze expand and grow,—
Higher it rose, fresher and brighter waved—
But oh ! rude blasts of cold Unkindness, keen
Satire, cutting Neglect, bitter, biting
Calumny, blighted its radiant hue—
It withered, drooped, and died.—
Oft, oft is Genius nipp'd by words
More freezing than frost, by looks colder than
Ice, and keener than the sword !

CALM SUMMER NIGHT.

Calm Summer night! God's blessing hovers o'er,—
   Tired of the Day, Toil's weary watches cease;
Care finds repose, his throbbing fevered brow
   Fanned by the spirit-wings of holy Peace;—

Flowers have folded their bright glossy cups,—
   As by a spell from some enchanter's wand
Their heads they droop; and welcome silence creeps
   With noiseless footfall over all the land;

The clear young Moon is smiling o'er the earth,—
   The wavy clouds are white as ocean foam,—
The stars look down so bright and tenderly,—
   Glimpses of glory from th' Eternal home,—

The aspen leaves move—move as in a dream—
The lake is sleeping in its pebbly bed;
The moon-rays gleam adown the village street,
Gleam on the church, and where repose the Dead;

Silent as thought the gentle dew descends,
As in olden time did manna from above;—
Earth seems dreaming of a happier clime
Holy and beautiful, where all is love;—

Rest weary world! Heaven is watching o'er thee,
Oblivious of all sorrow, rest in bliss!
Dream till the Hours gild the orient oceans,
And ruddy Morning wakes thee with a kiss.

WORDS.

Oh, WORDS are mighty !—Links of love that years
   Have formed into a bright and firm-wrought chain,
Which Time, nor Chance, could neither rust nor break,
   Are riven oft by words, which some call *vain*—
Feelings that with the buried dead would rest
   Till the Archangel's rousing note is heard,
Have started back, swift as the lightning's wing,
   And lived again, at breathing *Of a Word !*—

Oh, Words are mighty !—fiery burning thoughts
   Go forth from out the mind, and form a stair
Up which the soul goes journeying back to God,
   The noblest aspirations, Man calls *prayer*—

127

Words, sighing words,—Heart-words may give us life,
 And kindle hope full oft in dying eyes—
When the poor Thief hung bleeding on the Cross,
 They oped for him the Gates of Paradise.

Oh, Words are mighty!—The high pomp of state,
 And regal thrones—though guarded round with
  swords—
Have tottered to the ground 'neath Ruin's fire,
 Lit at the flaming torch of angry words—
And blood hath deluged many a smiling land,
 Where death lurked watching like a bird of prey,
When thoughts unuttered rankled at the heart,
 And Right and Wrong have stood like beasts at bay.

Words are not idle; no!—the ruddy cheek
 Will, at a word, turn white as driven snow;—
And oftentimes hot mantling blood will rush
 And crimson the pale face from neck to brow.
Words, call dark horror from its hidden deeps—
 Words, wake sweet music from the heart's mute
  chords;
Bring back old tones of by-gone melody
 To soothe us—Speak not then of idle words;

Oh, they are mighty !—for they own a power
  Unfathomed, fathomless, as ocean caves—
Associations strong as rushing tides,—
  Happiness clear and bright as sun-kissed waves ;
Remember ever, words can deeply wound,
  Can cleave firm hearts like sharp keen-edged swords ;
Can forge a dagger, or a bond of love—
  Pause, pause then, ere you utter " idle words ! "

VICO.

GREAT soul ! What seekest thou through the long night,
  Bending in rapt attention o'er the page
Which hollows thy dark eye, and dims thy sight,
  And gives unto thy youth the form of age?
Dost hope from thy lone, humble garret room
  To trace a name on History's mighty scroll?
To rend the veil of hoodwinked custom's gloom,
  And the fair characters of Truth t' unrol?
Foreseeing days thy thought high honour wins,—
  Days when the noble shall explore the mine
Of Knowledge—Though thy feeble body thins,
  And the keen eye grows keener—The divine
Soul still grows stronger,—and the thoughts which spring,
  And startle those around to sudden awe—

Seers shall see; and future poets sing,
  Thy words and systems an acknowledged law.

Ah me! To think the petty cares of life
  Should vex and mar a spirit such as thine;
To think, when Ignorance and Wrong were rife,
  E'en thou shouldst bow to men whose corn and wine
O'erflowed their garners—For thy loved at home,
  Thy wife and little ones, perforce might pine
And find no friend but thee 'neath Heaven's bleak dome
  Would give them succour—Yes, thy mental power,
    Thy subtlety of vision, in that hour
    Must needs be bartered oft, rich thoughts be led,
    And wrested, ay, and sold for daily bread.
And all for Knowledge—Knowledge was, I ween,
  The ladder which the Patriarch beheld—
Its base on the cold, common earth was seen,
  Its crest by Heaven's own bright arch upheld—
Angels ascending, and descending thence,—
  The marvellous inspirations which oft come;
Prophetic wisdom, songs, and visions, whence
  The soul holds commune with its spirit-home.

Footsore and weary thou didst travel on;—
  No leisure had thy life in lands unkind;

Footsore and weary—yet, when thou wert gone,
　Thy guiding words still led aright the blind
Dark erring world—Though pillowed on a stone,
　The active brain beheld, through murkiest night,
The glorious ray of knowledge, all thine own—
　Claimed kindred with the great, the brave, and free,
Then backward sped to the Eternity!

DREAMLAND.

THE firelight dances on the wall—
 Sitting in this familiar room,
I sadly lift dark memory's pall,
 And strive upon the gathering gloom,
Through mists of tears, once more to trace
The features of a much-loved face.

Often I try that voice to hear;
 That musical, low, pleasant tone—
But painfully upon mine ear
 The silence falls—alone, alone!
No sound throughout the long, blank day
Tells me she hovers o'er my way.

Last night, in sleep, I saw her stand
    Within our honeysuckle bower—
A pale white lily in her hand ;
    It seemed the tranquil evening hour—
So calm, as though to earth were given
A foretaste of the bliss of Heaven.

Sweet land of Dreams ! no clouds, no tears
    Bedim the brightness of thy sky—
The lingering shadow of the years
    Unknown, unheeded, pass thee by—
Time hath no power to destroy
Thy denizens, or blight their joy !

There, the long-lost, beloved ones come—
    There, clasp we many a vanished hand,—
There, gathered round the hearth of home,
    Meet once again its parted band ;—
Oh ! sad to break sleep's magic chain,
    To leave that hallowed spot,
Never to meet those forms again,
But roaming o'er Life's stormy main,
Find one thought ever haunt the brain,
    The thought that *they are not !*

CAMBRIA.

"Breathes there the man with soul so dead
Who never to himself hath said,
This is my own, my native land!"
(Lay of the Last Minstrel.)

Awake, harp, for Britain! Blest isle of the ocean!
Lulled by the waves' never-ceasing commotion,
   Still chanting of Freedom;—The theme
Of the lone Harper, Wind, as his trembling hands smite
The forest-oak harp on a wild wintry night—
Thy glistening leaves, and birds through the grove,
Exult in the chorus of Freedom and Love
   Echoed forth by each sea-bound stream.
Thy cliffs, as if touched by a silvery wand,
Rise white as bright light; thy strong bulwarks so grand,
   O Albion, fair land of the Free!—

135

Thy fertile green valleys; thy mountains sublime
That rise to the clouds unmouldered by Time,—
Thy cascades and streams; all *these* I love well,
But my spirit is linked by a rapturous spell
    To thee, ancient land of Cymru!

Thou once home of Bards! mighty, noble, and bold,
Who sang of enchantments and legends of old;
    Of chivalry, heroes, and war—
May thy osiered vales be free from all ills,
As the untrodden snow on the brow of thy hills:
Romance stands inscribed on each flowery dell,
Tranquillity breathed from each bud's drooping bell;
    May nought this tranquillity mar;
But Religion with Peace and Science combine,
And Wisdom, and Honor, and Justice entwine
    A wreath that shall evermore shed
Its influence o'er valleys and mountains sublime
That triumphantly rise, unmouldered by Time—
Though *all* Britain be dear—at Cambria's name
My bosom is kindled with patriot flame,
    Thou land of the glorious Dead!

Bright cradle of Song! Dear old country, thy name
Emblazoned for ever, exalted by Fame,

On History's page shall remain ;—
How thy dauntless bold heroes, of old, bravely fell
For their country and Freedom ; Renown their deeds tell,—
Let each child of Cymru adore and revere
His ancestors' spirit ; and valiantly rear
     His banner in Liberty's fane :—
For his own " Cymraeg" tongue, as his cheek burns with
     pride,
May each son sweetly blend affection's deep tide
     With zeal for the land of " Gwalia ;"
Brave valiant dead Cymry ! Bards ! Shades of our Sires !
May your faithful, your firm, your unsubdued fires,
Your lofty wild spirits, your magical muse,
Still glow in *our* souls, their influence diffuse
     Inspiration's wand over Cambria !

SUNGLINTS AND SHADOWS.

LIKE soothing sounds of balmy winds,
   Or wavelets of a river,
Thought steals softly o'er the mind,
   Still moving, moving ever—
Bright day of June, in musing mood
   I sat in that antique room,
While the old clock ticked the moments
   Of a sunny afternoon—
Outside, tall poplars' trembling leaves
   Danced lightly in the breeze,—
The grass, like mimic billows, stirred
   'Neath those rich-foliaged trees—
      I watched the restless shadows
         Flit o'er the chequered floor,
      Bright and joyous sunlight
         With shadows dancing o'er !

And thought how upon History's page
  Recorded acts of Life—
Scowled on by the grim foes of man,
  Famine, Death, War, and Strife
Move, darkling night-spots chasing back
  The glory-lights of Truth—
Still they appear, and disappear
  Like waking dreams of Youth—
Sunglints of Peace, Prosperity,—
  Joy-dancing, radiant gleams,
When swords are sheathed, and frowning brows
  Grow bright as Morning's beams—
      And thought returned and rested
       On that polished oaken floor
     Where the shadow chased the sunglint,
       Light and shadow o'er and o'er—
Old Time, where are the monuments,
  The temples rich and rare
Which ancient nations proudly saw
  Piercing the viewless air?
Are they those hoary shattered heaps
  Where Chaos fixed his throne—
Gaunt Ruin and Oblivion laugh
  Among, and claim their own?—

But see, new structures stately rise,
  And Builders build, and Peace smiles on,
And in magnificence arrayed,
  The New stands where the Old is gone—
The Jackall howls o'er a dreary waste,
  But Cities rise afar—
Where forest wildernesses waved,
  Rolls Trade's triumphal car ;—
      Still the poplar shadows gaily waved
        Across the oaken floor—
      Bright and joyous sunglints,
        With darkness dancing o'er.
Oh! summer of the human mind;
  The Intellectual sun
Shines o'er a land, and mighty thoughts,
  Soul's heaving waves, roll on—
Poet, Statesman, Orator,
  Philosopher, and Sage
Arise, like Stars in Heaven's blue,
  Lighting the happy age—
But stealthily the shadow creeps—
  The glorious Sun goes down ;
Another Age in other lands
  Soon hails the light its own ;—

And o'er the great Humanity,
 As on that oaken floor,—
Chasing beamy sunglints,
 Are shadows dancing o'er.
From the first dawn of infant Life,
 That like a tiny stream
Flashes and sparkles onward to
 Bright Childhood's happy gleam,—
To the rushing Life, that river-like
 Still gathers in its course
Th' experience of the weary years;
 The strong, soul-powerful force—
That tide of Being, surging tide,—
 That flowing, ebbing sea,
Now heaving, ever heaving back
 To the Eternity—
  The shadow with the sunshine
   Flashes, plays, and flashes o'er,
  Like the shadow of the poplar leaves
   On the antique oaken floor.
Life ! Life Past ! Life Present !
 Hope, Despair, Love, Hate,
Are the sunshine and the shadow
 That dance above thy gate ;—

While the blithe Bird of Joy yet sings
  Somewhere up in Life's tree,
Through darkness and discord listen
  To the distant melody—
On, on the Eternal ages glide,
  And Sin, in dismal dearth,
Chequers the golden light of Truth,
  As it smiles o'er the fallen Earth.—
Still waved the glistening leaves, and oh,
  Not an idle tale they told,
But a type they seemed of the Right and Wrong;
  The War, ever new, ever cld—
      Then wave ye leaves in your wildering
        dance
       O'er the polished oaken floor;
     Smile on, smile on ye sunglints
       Chase the shadows o'er and o'er !

How oft in the dim night, when tired and worn
　　With multifarious petty cares which make
　　The sum of many a daily life, I wake
Ere the glad East shows one bright streak of morn,
　　To hear thy voice in Fancy's musing ear
Repeat some happy strain of love and hope,
　　Calming each anxious palpitating fear—
While the lorn heart expands, as flowers ope
　　Their eyelids to the day—An Orphic song
Is that sweet voice—which wakes to joy the throng
　　Of shapeless shadowy thoughts, and words which fain
Would make a chaos of the weary brain.

LLANSTEPHAN CASTLE.

OVER thy mouldering walls
Hath crept the silent shadow of Old Time ;—
Where the harp of old awoke the bardic rhyme,
Whistles the wind through desolated halls ;—
Proud of its might it shakes the crumbling stone
    Where the green ivy-plant hath taken root ;
    And a few lone tufts of wall-flowers shoot
To deck the pile ; and wafting o'er the bed
Where sunk to rest the crowd of nameless Dead,
    Each wild breeze scatters 'round the fragrant bloom,
    Like sweetest incense 'bove the heroes' tomb ;—
Hast thou no tale, old Ruin hoary,
To tell th' inquiring children of To-day—
Recalling ancient years, ere thou wert grey,

Heroic song or legendary story ?—
Or deeds remembered by thy ramparts high
When Meredith withstood the Norman train ?—
Canst show no trophy of those days gone by ?
The Victor's shout ; the Vanquished's cry of pain
Recall ?—Who reared upon the hill's steep brow
The frowning battlements I stand on now,
Where from the turret's height the watchman's eye
Descried the rolling bay, the land, the sky ;
Saw the Invader's dreaded vessels sweep
Like white winged birds across the foaming deep ?—
The years have fled—and trackless as the Sea
The course the ages took to Eternity—
The Past is dumb—and dim as the To-Be ;—
That thou art here, a ruin—all we know ;
Builder, Bard, Warrior, dust to dust ere now.

SHALL MY SOUL MEET THINE?

In the twilight grey
  I watched for thee—
And mused, and sadly mused
  On what must be ;—
Lamp-lit streets grew gay,
  Glad ones passed along—
But my thoughts were far
  From the throng.

A dark day will come,
  It cometh soon ;
My soul shall soar away
  Beyond the moon ;

Beyond the moon and stars
   Heaven's portals shine—
My heart for ever asks,
   Shall my soul meet thine?

Time's glad years shall pass—
   Earth will ring
With music—Seasons come,
   Winter—Spring;
When my head rests low
   'Neath the mould,
Wilt *thou* laugh, and sing
   As of old?—

Canst thou bring to mind
   May-day eves,
When birdlets chirped and sung
   'Neath the eaves?—
When thou wouldst fondly look
   Heart-love untold—
Canst thou bring to mind
   Eves of old?

Shall my soul meet thine?
   To leave thee here

'Mid sin, and pain, and woe,
　　And sorrow drear—
'Tis sad !—'tis sad ! Oh, think
　　When on thy way,
I'm watching still for thee
　　At twilight grey !

SORROW.

Is there no shelter in Sahara vast;
   No shadow of a rock along Life's way,
   Where man may rest him in the evil day
Until the storm be spent, the Simoom past?
   Must devastating tempests wild sweep o'er
   The crushèd heart—that never blossoms more?—
Whirled, like a leaf before the Autumn wind,
   Man, man, poor atom! seems of Circumstance
The sport—his plans, playthings for Fortune blind,—
   His holiest feelings blighted by the glance
Of withering change;—His treasures dear
   Garnered by the Great Reaper, where he may
   Nor see, nor follow;—Oh! along the way

Is there no place to fly to from despair?
There *must* be shelter—God hath told us where.

    With thoughtful brow he stood alone,
        But not to muse of fame—
    Philosophy with subtle tone
        His thoughts no more could claim;
    Often, of old, the starry skies,
    With all their silent mysteries,
        Had been a charmèd book,
        Upon whose page he loved to look;—
            But now—but now,
            With throbbing brow
He stands in speechless grief alone;
Pale as a form of sculptured stone—
For him the stars might cease to shine,
    The sun remain unrisen—
Nature unheeded droop and pine—
    Earth had become a prison,
And Time the chain to bind him here,
From all he valued and held dear.

    A day had worn—as days *will* wear,
        However dark or bright—

The first day since his Mary's eyes
  Had quenched their living light;—
The strong man trembled, all his heart
  Seemed melted into tears ;
That summer day had heaped on him
  The agony of years !
Yet it had been bright to the world,
  As other days of old—
Sunset crept up a western cloud
  And tipped its edge with gold ;—
Through the open window breathed
  Rich fragrant garden flowers,
And wandering humming bees were heard
  Returning through the bowers ;
But, ah ! without, though all was fair,
And tranquil in the calm soft air,
And that was a mansion rich and rare,
  Where the lone one stood with sobbing breath,—
Let him weep !   Let him weep !
For the one he lov'd, hard by doth sleep
  In the icy arms of Death !

What are pyramids of roses,
And all the joys which earth discloses—

All summer's golden smiles,
That with beams light up the isles—
When the keen, sure-pointed dart
Of sorrow strikes the heart,
With stifling breath
From the stringèd bow of Death?
More welcome now would be
The barren blasted tree—
The rude north-eastern wild-wind with its roar,
Lashing in fury the forest oak,
Whose branches writhe 'neath the cruel stroke;
And blustering along the shore—
Anything but the southern breeze,—
Anything but the balm
Of odorous flowers, in the garden bowers—
Anything but the calm!

Ah! Sorrow, why wilt thou enter in
At the gorgeous palace door?
Why wilt thou not seek some pallid wretch,
Stretched on straw on his cold mud floor?
No joys hath he, for thee to hide
In thy winding sheet of snow;
Stern Poverty hath been there, and laid

The pensive feelings low :—
Ah ! Sorrow, art thou the same to all ?
Dost thou come with the shroud and sombre pall?
    Yes, whether the inmates be rich or poor—
Lofty or lowly, in cabin or hall,
    Thou enterest at the door—
All pleasure, and all treasure,
    Becometh worthless, vain —
The heart must bleed, for care and clouds
    Return still after rain.

And that manly form with tearful eyes,
    Where in smiles he stood of old—
Looks with bursting heart to the azure skies,
    While the blood at his heart grows cold ;
And cries, in the depth of his deep despair,—
" Anything, Lord, but this scene so fair,
    Anything but this southern breeze ; "
    As he pressed his brow with feverish palm, —
" Wild storm and tempest and foaming seas—
    Something that will accord with pain—
    Lord, help me !—my words are mad and vain—
    Oh ! anything but this calm !"

HAPPINESS.

THE sunshine on the distant hill
To which the mind oft turns with longing gaze ;
The ignus-fatuus that deludes the weak
Unwary one to danger, gloom, and death ;—
Imagination's fairy-land of joy ;—
The silver lining hidden in the cloud—
The precious pearl in Life's rough troubled sea,
For which age after age dives deep—Alas !
But finds not ;—The dazzling light-winged butterfly
Of Childhood's day, o'er Freedom's flower-wreathed
Hedge-rows, flitting still, away, away ;—
The glorious Future—*ever a To-morrow ;*—
Oh, Happiness ! Sister of Peace and Rest,
Oh ! Angel Happiness ! Like tired Hagar

In the days of old, we are athirst,
We faint amid this thorny wilderness,
We die;—oh, Happiness! Oh, Angel Happiness,
Let fall one drop from thy rich brimming chalice
To cool our parchèd Souls—Be still, poor heart,
Waste not thy sighs in empty air, be still!
'Tis but a ghost thou pleadest to, the pale
Ghost of Joy, that walks this twilight world;
Happiness is not here; beyond, beyond,
It dwelleth evermore—Awake! it is
The dream of Earth—The atmosphere of *Heaven*.

ICONOCLAST.

Why didst thou come,
When everything around was calm and sweet—
With scornful eye and sacrilegious feet
Those blossoms rich to trample ; and with hands
So fell and cruel, snap the silvery bands
In the warm heart's own home ?

Too high for mortal worth,
On a bright pedestal the idol stood ;
She reared the symbols of the great and good
Around him ; and his love like some clear star
Guided her very soul—and from afar
Led the affections, like the Magi old,
To offer gifts, and adorations manifold—
And hail him blest among the sons of earth.

Then thou didst come—
With weird visage, and dark hints, and doubt,
Until the lamp of faith slowly paled out :—
The inward vision never more could mark
Kindness, or purity, or joy ;—The sun
Of Hope eclipsed ;—Life's future sands might run
Down unto Death ; and Lethè-ward with might
The heart might drift, and sink far out of sight.

Hast seen the mountain snow,
All white and beautiful—flake upon flake,.
Forming a fairy pyramid ; until the storm awake
And the rash fury of the north-wind blow,—
And all the splendid structure downward throw,
Deep, deep into the valley, over-cast,
Trodden and soiled ; until, dissolved at last,
It sinks into the earth below ?

.   .   .   .

Thus fell the Idol, 'round whose head once shone
The halo bright of goodness—one by one,
Love's hopes congealed ;—Thy face so cold and keen,
Caused icicles to form where flowers had been.
It was a dream perhaps—but it shall be
Not lost, but treasured up eternally ;

157

The Ideal of the heart, strong, bold, and free!
Standing still firm—Each fluctuating wave
Of error rolling from it—All joy, all truth,
Nestling within its tranquil bosom—Youth,
Innocence, and Joy lighting the eyes—
Relic of Man's primeval Paradise!

FOUND DROWNED.

I.

WOULD the restless briny billow
Never, never let thee rest?
Tossing on the sea's dark breast,
    Or rocky cave—
Sea-weed, shells, and sand thy pillow;
While loud storm-winds hoarsely rave
    Above thy grave.

II.

On the tawny shore at last,
'Neath the glaring eye of Day
Thrown; Corruption's ghastly prey—

Not a trace
Left to tell of what hath passed,—
All unknown thy kindred, place,
  Form and face.

III.

Did the fury of the storm
Sweep thee from the reeling bark?
Hurling thee through frowning dark—
  And in the foam
Of surges deep engulph thy form,—
Bearing thee where'er they roam,
  Far from home?

IV.

Hast thou friends?   They'll oft bewail
Thy long, long absence—tears will start,
When thunders roar, and lightnings dart—
  Anxious eyes
At morn, and eve, watch many a sail
Gleaming 'twixt the sea and skies,
  Till e'en hope dies!

V.

Haply oppressed by care and strife,

When seen but by the evening star,
Where rivers wind through lands afar—
  And willows dank
Droop o'er,—Thou mightst have bartered life
For death, beneath the echoing bank—
  And thither sank :—

VI.

Thy Life-tale never will be told—
Strangers wrap thee in thy shroud,
And thou shalt rest, far from the crowd,
  Where bird and bee
Make music in green churchyard old—
Unknown to all, thy bliss or misery,
  Save God, and thee!

A SUMMER STORM.

THE Lark drops down to the waving corn,
   As tired of its journey skyward—
Dark gather the shadows, thick and fast ;
   The cawing rooks fly homeward ;—
Shrilly pipes the wind o'er the dusky moor,
   While adown the mountain side
Lowing kine seek some sheltered bank
   Where the forest songsters hide—
The frightened thrush to the covert hastes
   And drops the struggling worm ;—
In passive silence Nature stands
   T' await the coming storm.

Now all is stillness, far and near ;—
But hark ! from yonder thorn I hear
   A low and trilling sound,—

Hoarsely murmurs the rising blast,
And the rain comes pattering thick and fast.
　　In music on the ground !—

Again from the thorn, the leaf-clad thorn,
Come those sweet strains—not low and lorn,
　　But a loud and happy song,—
Mysterious Bird, what is it wakes
Thy heart to joy, while dripping brakes
　　Shelter a tuneless throng ?—

Still with the Tempest-spirit's wail,
With the rain-drop's beat and the thickening hail,
　　Blends the voice of that tiny form—
And louder swells the gladsome song
As echoes still the notes prolong,
　　Till lost amid the storm.—

O happy Bird! would I like thee,
From fears and from dismal terror free,
Untouched by cares and ills of Life,
In the wild tempest's raging strife,
　　Though clouds my sky deform ;
　　When the golden light of Day
　　Is ebbing fast away,
　　Could sing amid the storm !

THE NIGHT IS DARK AND COLD.

Through heavy mist the old tower bell
    Swung slowly to and fro;
Its iron tongue told the midnight hour
    To the silent street below—
No star looked out on the realms of sleep,
    Oh, the night was dark and cold!
When a Soul wandered here, to live awhile
    On earth in human mould.

Many a dawn was ushered in,
    Long nights closed over day;—
Not 'mong the children's noise and jest
    In careless mirth and play;

With boyhood's artless ringing laugh,
  And boyhood's sparkling eye,
Was that child-soul found ; but taught, alas !
  To beg, or steal, and lie.

Roaming the busy crowded streets,
  Neglected and alone ;
Hearing no voice of sympathy,
  No guiding, warning tone—
For the callous Boy, Philanthropy,
  Methinks thine eye was dry—
And pious people stepped aside,
  With faint half-prayer, half-sigh.

Many a dawn was ushered in—
  Winter's cold, Summer's heat ;
And the Man had grown, hard Cunning's own.
  'Mid the tramp of busy feet—
That sullied Soul, begrimed, besoiled,
  Scarce bore trace of heavenly mould—
Oh ! must, must it perish, wand'ring there
  In the night so dark and cold ?

Those Evil-genii—Misery, Want—
  Will they not let him rest ?

And that fearful demon, love of Gold,
    Burning within his breast ;—
Law, that ne'er succoured him, what heeds he ?—
    Fears no crime, howe'er fell—
Hunted, condemned, that wandering Soul
    Lies doomed in a felon's cell.

And the years have fled like wingéd birds
    With wide-spread pinions fleet—
The old bell telleth the hour still
    Above the silent street.—
A wail is borne on the midnight wind,
    Like a solemn anthem rolled—
Mercy hath winged her way to Heaven.
    Oh, the night is dark and cold!

IT COMES NOT AGAIN.

It comes not again ! that thrill of love,
  Like gladsome meeting of billowy streams ; —
Never will dawn on the aching heart
  Lost joy-light, that faded like evening's beams ;—
You Sun goeth down o'er the purple hill,
  But a halo-promise will still remain ;
'Twill greet us to-morrow—our farewell *had* hope,
  But *its* morrow is past, and it comes not again !

It comes not again—I cannot meet
  Thy form 'mong the living ;—Thy household hearth
Marks a vacant seat,—and yet I seem
  To dream of thee, still, a being of earth ;
As tear-blind I grope through the ruined Past—
  I seek thee, loved, vanished one, and fain
Would linger and live the olden time,
  But it comes not again ! it comes not again !

167

WAR.

How long, how long, shall War with all its brood
    Of hideous evils, Famine, Sword, and Flame,
Scatter Humanity's great brotherhood,
    Despoil and Waste, for glory's empty name?
Spreading dark Ruin o'er once fertile lands
    Where Plenty waved in golden affluence—
While sturdy Labor droops with listless hands,
    Pining in want beneath its influence—
And Art bows down its head, and Poesy grieves,
    And Commerce' busy wheels are hushed and still
While Trade decays—War, cruel War, it leaves
    The land its rude breath sweeps, cheerless and chill—
Well may the Nations groan and islands dread
    The scourge which strews their shores with countless
    Dead.

LOST! LOST!

BRIGHT, bright
Gleam the waves in the wan Moon's silver light,
While the stars look down from the fields of night ;
Not a sound is heard the deep calm to break,—
Save by fits, some wandering sea-gull's shriek :

On Sea,
A trim ship rides the billows merrily,
The bluff helmsman is whistling cheerily,
And the home-bound crew speak of bliss on shore,
But ah ! land shall their eyes meet never-more;

Mark, mark
That spiral flame like a meteor—Hark !
Comes that wildering cry from yon swanlike bark?

"Fire! fire!" shouts the boatswain, "Fire!" echo the
    crew,—
Calm looks the Moon in her sea-mirror blue—

A wail
Floats on the breath of the sorrowing gale,
That is gently fanning the snow-white sail ;—
What fear! what confusion! what terror wild!
To the hissing deep waves, leap sire and child!

A plunge! Crash!—the fire-lit vessel sinks,
Hear echoing groans from her falling brinks:
The waters close over; the sea rolls on—
And the last of that gallant crew is gone!

Weep! Weep!
The morning dawns, but the mariners sleep
'Mong the weeds and the shells of the briny deep—
The loved and the loving have found a grave,
A dreamless rest in the shade of the wave!

LIFE'S PATHWAY.

Clouds hover over Earth's sunniest spot,
  Ever 'mid greenest bowers,
Cypress is twined with the roses of joy—
  Thorns amid brightest flowers.

Sunshine and gladness shimmering o'er
  The darksome passes of life,—
Aching hearts veiled with smiling lips—
  Calm eyes o'er inward strife.

Stony and rough for the pilgrim's feet
  Is the pathway everywhere ;—
Care haunteth city, forest, and field,
  E'en the solemn house of prayer.

Oh, have ye friendship?   Have ye heart-homes ?
  Guard them with thoughts, deeds, words—
For truly o'er Earth's fairest Paradise hangs
  The shadow of gleaming swords.

BLIGHTED HOPES.

As blossoms through the summer air
   Ambrosial odours shed,
When fairy-footed Morning starts
   From her billowy bed;—
As sparkling stars through midnight gleam,
   When some dark cloudlet opes,
Around his pathway clustering
   Came bright delusive hopes;—

Like dew-drops on the vernal grass,
   Like foam-bells on a stream—
Transient as they—alas! to fade,
   The glories of a dream—
A dream, no, *that* will calmly rest
   'Neath the Lethean wave,
But grisly phantoms, blighted hopes
   Rise from the Past's deep grave:—

Oh, Disappointment's sullen blast
 Scattered his joys apart,
And sere they lay beneath that wild
 Tornado of the Heart;
Loud did the hollow Past resound,
 Sad as the Night-wind's shriek
Above the shattered wreck, o'er which
 The waves their vengeance wreak.

'Twas sad to watch the gathering storm,
 Its clouds, and sorrow dark,
Low'ring, and all his hopes and joys
 Freighted in one frail bark!—
That little bark, to him more dear
 Than a rich argosy,
Fade from his sight amid the gloom
 Of dismal Destiny!

Ah! tempest-tost and rudderless
 The heart, once gay and fair,
Plunges adown the abysmal depths
 Of desolate Despair;—
Wan Reason like the Moon's pale light
 Glimmering o'er the scene;

173

A fragmentary ruin left,
   To show where joy hath been !

The bruiséd and storm-beaten pine
   May burst to bud again ;
But the fierce-riven, lightning scathed,
   Blasted will aye remain ;
Though healing showers and dews descend,
   Mild gentle zephyrs sigh
Above the branches, withering
   They bend, and bending die.

Thus to the stricken spirit, dews
   Of sympathy may come,—
Alas ! the heart's soft music chords
   For evermore are dumb.
The atmosphere of thought is dark,
   Earth, sky, below, above,
A blank—Dim sight alone beholds
   The blighted hopes of Love.

A STORMY DAY.

BLEAK, bleak and cold! ah, bitter cold!
  What could more bitter be?
'Neath the leaden sky of a wintry eve,
  Winds shrieking loud and hoarse,—
      Like a spirit lost,
      Loud wailing tost
  On the ocean of remorse :—
Rough winds that make earth groan and grieve
  And heave the mighty Sea!

Wild ruthless Wind! Ah, mighty Wind!
  Like a giant fierce at play—
Tossing huge oaks with thy unseen hand,—
  Scattering the forest's leafy band—

Then far away
O'er bluff and bay ;
Where the petrels shriek, and sea-mews flock,
Shrouding the dark-ribbed rugged rock
In clouds of foam and spray.

Up the dim valley, adown the lane—
Over the house-top high—
Whistling, and rattling the window pane,
Shaking with fury the church-tower vane,
Careering through the sky.—
Bleak, bleak and cold, ah ! bitter cold,
When ruthless storm-winds blow,—
Why waken the forests from wintry sleep?
Why rouse the dread rage of the briny deep?
Why make widows and orphans to wail and weep?
The God of the Wind doth know.

WE WILL NOT WEEP FOR HIM.

Away on the everlasting hills,
   In glory now
He sitteth—Shall we weep that Death
   Hath stilled that throbbing brow?

We will not heave deep sighs for him;
   Yet he was one to love—
One of the chosen pearls was he
   To deck Christ's crown above.

We will not weep for him,—On earth
   He could not stay—
Unto his glorious home he went,
   While yet 'twas day ;—

The leaves were green around his cot,
  And earth was fair ;
Yet to the Heavens his spirit fled,—
  His God was there.

Away on the everlasting hills—
  In glory now
He rests—Let us not weep—A crown
  Decketh the Victor's brow !

PLEASURE.

WE are as children gazing up the height
 Of some steep mount beneath the eye of Day,
Who fancy with wild feelings of delight,
 Heaven bends to touch the summit's line of grey—

So upward climb, led on by Thought's pale ray—
 The azure sky no nearer ;—Till with feet
All torn and bleeding,—sinking in the way,
 They find their hope a vain delusive cheat :—

Thus from the Present's plain, we see afar
 Th' untrodden Future rising with no frown
Ruffling its calm ; and Pleasure's beaming star,
 With lustrous splendour sparkling in its crown.

And so the dazzling meteor we pursue ;—
 Pleasure to grasp, o'er rugged pathways rove ;—
Ah ! as we seek, it still recedes from view,
 Ever in mockery rising clear above.

AN AUTUMN THOUGHT.

Flowers droop, decay, and no one mourns;
 No pity-breathing tone
Stays the rude touch of Autumn's blast
 When the last Sun-ray 's gone,
It whirls the pallid leaf to die
 Upon the plain alone;

And soon above the wintry grave
 Bloom the fresh buds of spring—
Thus, in forgetfulness Man rests—
 While smiling forests ring
With thrilling music—Friends beloved
 Grow calm;—The senseless thing

Sepulchred low—they mourn no more:—
 The dead leaf, let it lie,

And wither 'neath the grass—'Twere vain
  Longer to grieve and sigh ;—
Yes, let it rest.—And thus we fall,
  Forgotten thus we die !

A frail dead flower—A withered leaf
  Shed from its parent tree,
Lost 'mid the countless hosts of Death,
  Veiled in Eternity ;—
Yet would we wish to live alway,
  In some fond memory.

SONG TO DEJECTION.

Yes, 'tis an old, old tale of woe
  That " Man is born to trouble,"
That " Death will be a bless'd release,"
  That " Life 's a passing bubble "—
        But out, I say, upon the man
        Who, when misfortune meets him,
        Sits heaving sighs, with downcast eyes,
        And fluttering heart a-beating.

Look up, look up with dauntless brow—
  Shall Circumstance affright thee ?
No ! make it but a stepping-stone,
  Experience soon will teach thee
        The world will frown upon a man
        Who lets it see his sorrow ;

182

Then work in hope of sunny skies,
    And prosp'rous gales to-morrow !

A sturdy tree, when adverse winds
    Sweep o'er the trembling forest,
Will bend perhaps, but rise again
    And battle with the bravest ;—
        Dejection never saved a wreck,
          Or set a ship afloat—
        Will Grief build up a ruined house,
          Or change a thread-bare coat ?

Fate, Chance, my friend, are dreams that lull,
    And stay the wheels of Motion ;
Be Patient—Patience worketh Hope,
    And Hope incites to Action—
        Yes, out I say upon the man,
          Who, when misfortune meets him,
          Sits heaving sighs, with folded arms
        And fluttering heart a-beating.

ROLL ON, CLEAR STREAM.

Roll on, clear stream! Thy ripples wake
　　Old memories that have slumbered long;
Roll on, gay stream!　Thy singing wakes
　　The echo of another song.—

Old weary willows brooding there;
　　Old sedgy banks and rushes green—
Know ye the child—yet child no more,
　　Who comes to view this haunted scene?

Oft here, at stilly morn and eve
　　I heard the holy Sabbath bell
Borne softly over wood and wild—
　　Sighing amid this shady dell!

Long Summer days were far too short
　　To list among the foliage fair,
The blended sounds bird, bee, and brook
　　Poured forth in music on the air.

184

Bright golden Harvest-moons have set
  Beyond the hills; and many a Spring
Ripened to Summer, since I heard
  Thy brown wren chirp, and blackbird sing :—

As Silence wakens, when a voice
  Rouses her dim dark rocky caves,
Thought rises, clothes itself with words,
  At bidding of thy magic waves.

And merry voices of old friends
  Come from beyond the distant main,
Where river-like the Years have flown,—
  And Childhood's Morning dawns again!

And ruddy health smiles on each cheek;
  And roguish laughter lights each eye—
A gladsome little band, with no
  Horizon to Joy's cloudless sky.—

And far off clover-scented morns—
  With hum of insects in the flowers,
Are borne back in that silvery strain
  Of thine, to cheat the passing Hours—

Ay, cheat the Hours—for know since then,
  Reality with Argus-eyes
Peeped o'er the hills—and showed us there
  The grey horizon of Joy's skies;

And now we turn, and gaze behind—
  (Time hath put out that inner light)
And frighted by dim shadowy thoughts,
  We vex and strain the aching sight

To catch a glimpse, however faint,
  Of Future-land; and tip-toe stand
With sinking hearts :—Presumptuous Doubt
  Would tear the veil from Mercy's hand.

"It was," and " Will be," those are words
  Which happy Childhood never needs—
True, simple Gladness finds " It is,"
  Phrase rich enough, and nought else heeds.

Oh, in this world of gloom and change,
  Where all of earthly mould
Decay, thou seemest gay and bright
  Unchanging, never old !

Rounding the pebbles as they lie
  Within their crystal bed—
In peaceful joy, while thunders rend
  The storm-clouds overhead.

The stars smile from their azure heights
  At mirrored stars below ;
And Luna's placid face is there
  Gleaming through Winter's snow—

Or when the calm still Summer night
  Steals o'er the fragrant air ;
And all is hushed in sleep, thou art
  The only watcher there.

Thy lay like some prophetic voice,
  Back from the shades of death
Can call the Past,—and perished forms
  Re-animate with breath.—

Then roll, clear stream, and may my soul
  Mirror the light of Truth
As thou yon star ;—Roll on, gay stream,
  Type of perpetual Youth !

187

THE LOVE OF LIFE.

No silvery fringes edge the clouds to-night,
A dull dead haze closed the pale gate of Day,
And twilight merged to darkness unawares—
The Earth, clothed in a thin grey robe of mist,
Hears the low muffled music of the winds
Breathing in sadness through the leafless woods—

There is no gladness shimmering around—
Nought grand or terrible sublimes the scene ;
Yet Earth we love thee still ! Though seasons change,
And dark Decay robs thee of leaves and flowers—
Steals the bright foliage, leaving thee the thorns ;—
And birds forget to cheer thy drooping heart—
In Winter's snow, as in the Summer shine,
O Earth, our mother, we have always lov'd thee !

We cannot choose but drop a tear to think
A dark hour cometh, when these eyes must look
Their last on wood, and field, and flower ; and close,
Never to open more! Dark hour! when trees shall wave,
Warm Autumn suns tinge the glad golden grain,
And Winter nights grow radiant with stars,
And other eyes behold their glory, while
The clear cold moon smiles o'er our mould'ring graves.
     Then comes the wish to live
On, on, and on ! Humanity dreads Death—
Ay, and a thousand ills will brave t' evade
That mighty one—Sorrow, and pain, and grief,
May beat upon the Beggar's homeless head
All desolate and cold—Like Winter's storm
Howling around some lonely cot upon
A barren heath ; each gust more fiercely wild,
More ruthless than the last—Still threatening
To cast it to the ground, a roofless ruin—
But when th' exhausted tempest perishes,
And the bright Morning comes to paint anew
The landscape with his variegated hues—
We find the hut, though desolate, still there ;
And thus in bitterness, the poor crushed heart
Braves the keen withering blasts of Destiny—

Clinging to life, as some poor drowning fly
Clings to a blade of grass whirled round and round
The eddy of a waterfall.—

Misery, wandering homeless through the world,
Would scarcely wish to-night, in the dim dark,
To stretch his weary limbs and sleep, the last
Long dreamless sleep, e'en though he knew next morn
He'd wake to blissful glory!

LINES TO ——

Thou sayest thy pathway is often o'ershrouded,
  Clouds above and around thee portentously loom ;
Thou canst not perceive that Goodness and Mercy,
  God's bright-beaming love-lights, aye fringe the dark gloom;
Thy soul can expand beneath Night's starry wonders,
  Ecstatic can list to yon thunder-toned sea ;
And dost thou forget *The Presence* that formed them,
  Infinitude's King watcheth even o'er thee ?—

Now Decay's burning fingers have touched the green branches,
  And clutched the fruit-crown from Autumn's hoar head,
With wild frantic glee, as the old Year lay shivering,
  Despoiled of its riches, its garments—half dead ;
And soon it will die, and its funeral dirge
  Shall be piped o'er the mountains by voices unkind ;

191

But wrapped in its snow-shroud, 'twill hear not the surge
Loud-leaping the rock, nor the cloud-driving wind;—

Yet Earth from their trance shall wake frost-bound valleys,
When joy-gleaming streamlets are oceanward seen
Gaily dancing through meadows, and deep in old shadows
Of dim forests—boughs don their kirtles of green ;
When birds trill their glad notes, forgetful of dark days,
And dead leaves by violets are hidden,—like Care
Lost beneath Happiness—Heed thou their teachings,
 " Rise, mourn not the Past, while the Present is fair ;"—

Yes, the black night of trouble may close o'er the brightest
And sunniest day that e'er gladdened the ground,—
And o'er-head roll the Tempest-car, laden with lightning,—
The Sky's grand artillery boom deafeningly 'round,—
While Nature quakes awe-struck; but *Night* dawns to
 Morning.—
The eagle-like Clouds wing their swift way above—
O'er the distant horizon sweet sunbeams are gleaming,
While the leaf-stirring breeze softly sighs—"God is love."

Oh, Riches may fly, and Fortune frown darkly,
And, swallow-like, friends with summer depart ;

Pleasure prove but a mirage—the World's smiles delude
    thee,—
False lights, soon gone out in the midnight of heart;—
With the chill winds of Fate up-heaving Life's billows,
    Mayst thou yet find the gem—*Truth*, so precious and rare—
And still thou *hast* some one to live for, and love thee ;—
    Hope on then—thank God—and never despair ;

Life's sky *may* be darksome, but look, streaks of azure
    And bright tinted bows irradiate the gloom—
Life's path *may* be thorny ; but seek mid the *briars*
    Sweet blossoms of *kindness*, in purity bloom ;—
Oh, think then, when gazing on Night's deep world-wonders,
    Or Eternity's type—the broad boundless sea,—
Looking up, full of faith, through the mist-clouds of Error ;
    The King of Infinitude careth for thee !

A CHILD'S GRIEF.

SORROW touched a child's young heart
And made the ready hot tears start;
And the little bosom heave with many a sob and
    moan,—
For the night wore on to day,
And the mother, still away,
Came not to cheer and bless him with her loving
    tender tone.

But grief stays not with youth—
Sorrow, and pain, and ruth,
But touch it as with silken wings, then darkling pass
    away;
The Future bright and green,
With hopes and joys unseen—

Gilds the Present with bright haloes, that ever round it
 play ;—

 And ere the silvery glow
 Of another Moon's bright bow,
Fringed chequered Autumn's cloudy sky with beaming
 rays of light ;
 Like the wind above the grave—
 Or light ripples on the wave—
The memory of Death became a passing dream of
 night.

Stay, stay, thoughts of bright blissful days,
  In all your golden sheen
Gild the lone twilight of our after life,
  And keep our memories green !

    Visions of Happiness,
      Visions of Joy and Truth,
    We grieve to see thee pass away like mist—
    O'er the hill-tops of youth ;—

Smile, smile, be with us yet awhile,
  Gladden our hearts, until
Through griefs, and cares, and worldly strife,
  We climb life's rugged hill.

A DREAM.

Oh, what strange sights,
Strange thoughts, mis-shapen deeds, and scenes uncouth,
Old Morpheus twists into his vagaries
When he unfolds a tale, and cheats the brain
E'en to believe it true.—One night, 'twas in
The Winter wild, when all the elements
Seemed leagued with the grim Spirit of the storm,
To laugh at human weakness :—When mine ear
Was dulled with ceaseless pattering of rain,
And roar of angry winds, I fell asleep—
And soon beheld a temple huge and bold,
More gorgeous than the fabled structure raised
By Bagdad caliph in the olden time.
Vast throngs of men, women, and children came

With eager faces pressing onward still
Towards the gates—I entered with the rest,—
And questioning old Morpheus of the name
Of the great Deity they worshipped there,
He told me 'twas the modern Moloch's fane ;
And daily, hourly, evermore he drained
His willing victim's life-blood :—There on high
Rose in the midst an altar glorious,
Glowing with splendour like unto a Sun ;
The people flocked around—some knelt
Before it ; and some cut themselves with knives
Of Crime and dark Ignominy ; and some
Tortured the others ;—There were cries and groans,
And muttered curses from the fallen too ;—
Ground in the dust beneath Oppression's heel.
Oh, fearful sight !—One poor crushed man I saw,
Goaded to madness with the fearful doubt
He'd never reach the Idol where it stood :—
I saw one with firm step walk to the front
And with hot irons sere his Conscience out.
(At this the Oracle seemed truly moved)
A few there were who came, bared their pale brows,
And gave the teeming brain as offerings—
Some tender-hearted Fathers laid their sons

Upon the altar, till the blood oozed out—
And Mothers too, who gladly brought, with smiles,
Their meek-eyed daughters to the sacrifice.
I saw a stately lady, with white hands
Pluck her own heart out, and with beaming eyes
Present it to the Idol as its due :—
But oh ! the crush, the shrieks, the yells
Of myriad voices struggling ouward still !
The groans of gasping wretches, yielding their
Last breath in the great struggle at the shrine :
Many were slaves ; I could distinctly hear
The harsh loud clanking of their heavy chains.
I asked my guide to tell me, in what land ?
Beneath what sky ?—among what race of men,
Such lavish gifts of brain, of heart and blood,
Were given by such eager votaries?
Some word— But my Interpreter had flown,
And Day had dawned ; and I was there alone—
Thanking kind Fate my " lines had fallen " here,
" In pleasant places," where fair Truth and Love,
Mercy and Goodness are the only shrines
At which men bow and worship ;—Full of faith
In God, and in each other—Blest indeed !

Blow, blow, wild winds! and spend the dreary darkness
    In mournful wailings round the lonely shore—
I lie awake and hear loud echoes float
Through the wide air in many a deafening note
    Which vex my restless spirit more and more.

I could not bear this strife with unseen phantoms
    That mock the heart with whisperings of woe—
Forebodings dark filling the dreary chasm
Of distance ; haunting the still deep abysm,
    Did I not know that when the bright skies glow

With June's soft warmth—and blossoming roses crown
    The year with blushing beauty glad and gay,
Thou wouldst return again, and smile and make me blest,
And with sweet Hope I try to calm th' unquiet breast
    And while the weary, weary hours while thou art
        still away;

ELIZA.

Oh, how sweet it was to linger
  With no care to cloud the brow,
And watch the grey clouds kindle
  With evening's parting glow !—
Heaped pile on pile, and all alight
  Seemed Day's funereal pyre—
While the round red Sun sunk slowly down,
  Like some great world on fire !

Or when like pious Priestess
  To some holy festal rite,
The pale calm Moon ascended
  The azure vault of night ;—
While the tall fir trees 'bove our heads
  Like waving banners gleamed,
Rejoicing in the gentle light
  Which through their branches streamed ;

We stood, and watched star after star
  Come forth with twinkling beam—
And converse held that sweetly touched
  On many a lofty theme ;—
Our opening thoughts grew each like each,
  As on the self-same bough,
Twin spring-buds bloom serenely—
  They've long been severed now !

But yet my soul would wish to hold
  Communion sweet with thine—
Canst thou, bright Spirit, from the skies
  Still see and feel for mine ?
Thou, glorified amid the Blest,
  I, a poor pilgrim here,
Would fain believe, from that far, high,
  Unclouded, blissful sphere,
The love which lighted earth for me
  With undiminished glow,
Although unseen, sheds its pure light
  O'er my life-path below.

The landscape now seems tinged with gloom
  From sorrow's dismal shade—

All that remains of thee on earth
In one small spot is laid !
The Autumn leaves fall o'er it,
And the pensive robin trills
His latest song, as sunny days
Are fleeting o'er the hills.

Eliza, tender fragile bud !
It was the hand of love
Removed thee from the alien land
Unto thy home above ; '
Yet tears of grief were shed for thee—
Bitter as falling showers,
Bursting above the lowly grave
Of summer's withered flowers.

Still, still we mourn, but Faith discerns
Beyond Death's starless night,
The smiling beams of radiant dawn—
The holy Land of Light !
And my heart will hush its murmurings,
Still sorrow's rising swell ;
Hope whispers we shall meet, when Time
And I have bid farewell !

"A BROTHER BORN FOR ADVERSITY."

Honest, and learned, and liberal he was ;—
With such a magnanimity of mind
As in a great man would have made him greater,
But he was poor,—And magnanimity
In a poor man is seldom spoken of :—
Many bright visions, many joyous dreams,
Illumined each brightening morrow of his boyhood;—
The lore of ancient sages soon became
Even as his daily food—The hunger
Of the deep soul seemed never satisfied—
The visible, the gross, the tangible,
The merely physical he could not take
Into his warm affections, and his heart
Still alway seemed Imagination's home ;—
He was ambitious, but it was to ascend

Unto the heights where Science leads the mind
To learn its secrets and its mysteries.—
Ambitious too, that the kind Muse should come
And smile and be the Angel of his home.—
High sounding names and all the appendages
Of rank were naught to him—He could have stood
Before a King—a good King, unabashed,
His equal—His keen eye beheld at once
The Soul through outward Clay—And though a crown
Glittered upon the forehead of a fool
He could not bow to him, even outwardly—
He never cringed, nor fawned, nor flattered,
Meaner souls might climb the slippery stair
Of social eminence and be applauded great
By the unthinking crowd—He'd struggle on !—
The Upas-tree of evil never cast
Its blighting shadow o'er his noble soul,
Or cooled the kind warmth of his genial heart
Which glowed with faith, and hope, and charity—
Noxious and vile as Circe's were, he swore,
The draughts poured forth from Pleasure's ready hand
Which the gay giddy world drank, yea, and praised :—
Sights wondrous, gaping multitudes applause,
(Refinement and good taste apart) he held

Were treason to the faculty divine
Which the Creator breathed into his last
And noblest creature.—In the seat of scorn
He never sate—True Piety, though poor
And unadorned—Goodness wherever found,
His inmost soul would rise to venerate ;
But Cant, Deceit, and Falsehood—varnished lies,
Though tricked in gorgeous trappings, he denounced
With kindling cheek and unmistakeable
Enthusiasm.—And the subtle arts—
But ah ! why speak of him ? and of the ire
Which shook a spirit long, long since at rest ?
Why speak of him indeed?—He never ploughed
The briny deep for gainful merchandise,
Nor scattered grain in wide deep furrowed fields,
Nor delved into the bowels of the earth,
Nor took a place within Trade's busy mart—
Nor with red hands hewed out a path to fame ;
Speak not of him—Poor and unfortunate !

And yet *he* toiled !   And that most manfully
'Mid the great world of Science and of Art—
On through the lengthening years without a pause,
Toiling with firm endurance, while the cares
And pains and woes of life fell drop by drop,

As fall light showers upon the waving tree ;
But Winter came—And the cold storm and rain
Beat wildly on him—Then—ah ! nevermore
Could he hold up that poor defenceless head.

He lived—Idealist, what did he get ?—
Neglect, privation, sorrow, pain, and debt :—
He died—no friend was nigh, no pitying tear
Dropping above his cold unconscious bier—
He died—Serenely sinking to repose
From wan disease, the soul sublimely rose—
Even to the last, with heart bowed, and bent knee,
He still could praise the God who made him free !

BOOKS.

Books, the Past with all its treasures to the Present's eye unroll,
And we see the mystic old world rising like an open scroll
Whereon man hath traced the longing, grand aspirings of the soul.

While Time, that mighty Despot, beneath its cruel sway
Age after age, like crested waves, fast eddying hurls away—
Yesterday's City vast becomes a ruined waste to-day.

Noble works of ancient ages—Temples, towers of massive stone,
Old Nineveh, Palmyra, Troy, have long been overthrown;—
But these monuments of ages are yet firm, are yet our own.

How we love their sweet rich glory as it bursts upon our sight—
Unshrouded by the gloomy years—Truth's ever-earnest light—
Like those stars which gleam above us through the clouds of
    Winter's night!

The conquering of Conquerors ! Noble and great were ye !
Who wielded Freedom's sword-like pen, who taught minds to be
  free—
Who graved your high immortal thoughts upon Humanity !

Rich stores are here, rich relics, flowers and plants from every clime—
And strains of Bards, who singing soared up Heaven's heights
  sublime—
Ay, gems worthy the adorning of the jewelled crown of Time !

From the troubled tossing scenes of Earth those great King-souls
  have fled—
Dissolved into its kindred dust, each busy throbbing head—
Yet I can muse and commune with the distant and the Dead—

Old books, in your diversity ye still speak of a whole—
As though through the Eternal gates a ray of glory stole,—
Shining on all, or faint, or bright, the One great human soul.

Like mystic oracles ye speak ;—As when from some far height
The rushing dash of waters strikes the deep still calm of Night—
Ye wake the soul entranced that waits for spirit rays of Light.

THE END.

www.ingramcontent.com/pod-product-compliance
Lightning Source LLC
Chambersburg PA
CBHW020610030726
47497CB00007B/2165